WEA
OR NUT

Jane Waller

Publishing details

ISBN No 978-1-913136-71-0

The cover illustration shows Lundy, the Cook, and Hebrides, the Black
Witch, chasing the Fair Weather Kittiwake in the Heligoland Kitchen.
Heligoland Hall is in the distance, situated beneathe a LOW over the Irish
Sea ... and the Weather is also depicted with spiral isobars and a Cold Front.

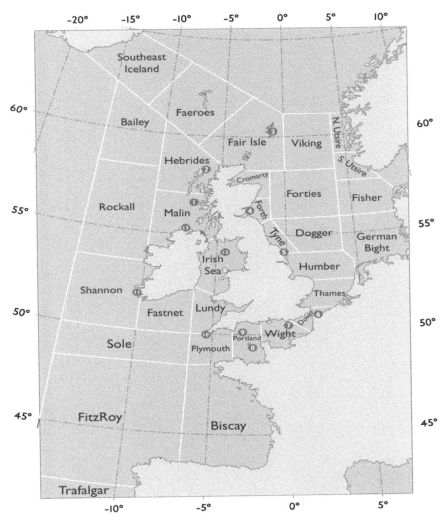

N.B. *The shipping area of Finisterre was changed to Fitzroy on 4th Feb, 2002*

Part One
Heligoland

The Cast of
WEATHER or NOT

At Heligoland Hall
THE FOUL WEATHER-MAKERS

HUMBER : Captain of the Castle; outsize hailstones & snowflakes

MALIN-the-BAD : ice, cold & grey clouds

GERMAN BIGHT : Castle Genius; synoptic charts.

HEBRIDES-the-BLACK WITCH : lightning, wrecking & fog

LUNDY : the Castle Cook.

VIKING-the-THUNDERER : thunder & thunderbolts

SOLE-the-DOLEFUL : rain

BISCAY-the-BLUSTERY : wind

(Shannon and Wizard Cromarty expired)

Foul Weather Birds

Stormy Petrels, Skua, Razorbills, Cormorants, Shags and Gulls

Chapter 1
Grandpa's Secret

For days now, an annoying wind had howled and whirled itself up and down the open chimney of the Midwinters' house, as if searching … hunting around. It chased the falling rain-drops, smudging them down inside, creating long runnels of ancient sticky soot.

'Rain. Rain. Rain. When will it ever stop!'

Wendy and her mother pushed their umbrellas against the downpour as they battled through deep puddles towards the hospital, where Grandpa had been taken the day before.

Today, Matron had phoned to summon them to his bedside, as he was now "very poorly, and not long for this world."

Mrs Midwinter said her goodbyes first, then tearfully beckoned Wendy to do the same while she spoke to Matron.

But, as Wendy reached his bedside, Grandpa Midwinter heaved himself painfully on one elbow to beckon her close.

A look of panic covered his face. He was summoning all his remaining strength to speak to her.

'Wendy, listen – listen carefully – you have to do something for me - something of the utmost importance.'

Wendy bent closer. What remained of his voice sounded so urgent; so harsh.

'I've been Guardian of a very large book - a Tome – which I smuggled out of Germany during the Second World War. I lodged it for safety a little way up our chimney. It's wrapped in a piece of old parachute silk. Promise me, Wendy … promise me faithfully you'll take it to Mr Allbright, the new Chief Weather-Man at the Exeter Weather Station. This Tome is highly dangerous … must be kept safe … … at all cost. Tell no-one. I was about to take it myself during the opening of the 'Weather Exhibition' at the Met Office tomorrow … but it was reaching for it inside the chimney that brought on my collapse.'

'What's in it that's so special, Grandpa?'

'The weather's inside it,' he answered in a strained voice, as he lay back exhausted. Wendy leaned closer still. She could hardly hear … 'All the weather … how it is made.'

'I don't understand how can it do that? Explain a bit more to me, Grandpa … please …'

But her Grandfather, having told his secret, had passed silently away, his face relaxed at last into a look of great relief.

Mrs Midwinter clutched Wendy's hand tightly for comfort as they splashed their way homewards.

'Oh dear, it's been such Foul Weather now for a whole year. I can hardly bear it! And to happen just when Grandpa's award for 'A Lifetime's Weather Research' was going to be presented to him tomorrow … but I suppose I'll have to collect the award on his behalf. I'm glad you're coming with me, Wendy - you love everything about the weather – just as Grandpa did. Oh dear! How I long for those days when the weather was so fine I could hang my washing outside to dry…'

Wendy, however, was not really listening. She was still puzzling things out as she walked along.

Yes, Grandpa had been the Chief Weatherman at the Met Office when it had been up in Bracknell. And his weather-research was so important, that when the Met Office moved down to Exeter, their whole family had been moved down to Fitzroy Road, not far away from his work.

It felt very important for her to carry out his last request. She'd promised … and she'd try to do it as best she could.

So, that night, after her mother, worn out with grief, had gone up early to her room, Wendy crept downstairs to carry out Grandpa's wish. There, in the living room, was their old electric fire, prised from its position in front of the chimney-place, ready to be replaced later in the week by the fashionable log-burning stove her Mother had saved up for.

And it had been this fire-place being opened up, she realised, which was why Grandpa had been forced to find a new safe hiding-place for his important 'Tome'.

Wendy sighed as she tied her mother's headscarf around her head and, with a torch, dutifully began scrabbling around, searching their chimney for Grandpa's parcel.

Above her, that horrid cold draught was blowing down again, whining and moaning around her head, blustering into her face while she searched, causing soot to fall into her eyes, which had already gone red from crying.

Then a loud 'Squark' caused further soot to cascade, as a trapped bird flew past her and began blundering around the room.

Wendy stopped her search to open the front door, managing to shoo the bird outside. The poor thing looked like some sort of sea bird – a Stormy Petrel perhaps - but completely covered in soot.

'I wish I'd been born a sea-bird,' she thought, as she eventually found and extracted the parcel, wedged behind what looked like part of an old bread-oven … 'then I wouldn't be trapped indoors like this day after day with all this foul weather.'

Sooty footsteps followed Wendy as she carried the parcel upstairs to her room. The Tome was rather heavy and brought her down to earth from imagining herself a sea-bird, gliding effortlessly over the ocean on outspread wings, buffeted by all kinds of wind, while looking down at the coastline of the British Isles below.

Wendy unwrapped the parachute parcel on the floor – and there it was - Grandpa's precious Tome. It had a dark navy blue cover, and looked quite boring.

'Cabalistic Weather-signs and symbols.
Johann Heinrich Lambert 1772.'

As she traced the name of the book with her finger, its cover appeared to change to a more pleasant green – inviting her to look inside.

On thick crackly pages were ancient runes; charts; diagrams with hand-painted margins … all looking hundreds, even thousands of years old. 'What are these weird weather-symbols? They're very beautiful - but a bit scary as well … almost like magic spells?'

Then Wendy came across what she knew were her Grandfather's comments, with various bits of equation he'd tried to work out in the margins …

This made her cry again … but … how peculiar! Her tears, when they hit the pages, fizzed, popped, and dried out completely.

By then, Wendy was feeling too tired to continue crouched down on the floor, so she carried the Tome into bed with her and propped it against her knees to continue looking. She remembered how, over the years, her Grandpa had taught her nearly everything he knew about the weather.

She particularly loved listening to The Shipping Forecast whenever she could …"Fair Isle, Viking, Hebrides … stormy winds backing south-westerly. Visibility, poor," and so on.

(Grandpa had told her that her first spoken word had been "Altocumulus").

Then Wendy came across a page in his own hand-writing, tucked neatly inside the Tome – it was the fairy story he used to tell her when she was very young and tucked up warm in bed:

"Once upon a time there was a great glittering castle suspended in the air above the middle of the Irish Sea. Many years past, a pair of twin Wizards: Wizard Wight and Wizard Cromarty, were born in this castle. Their parents, Captain Humber and his Irish wife, Shannon, could hardly tell one twin from the other, being alike as the two halves of a hinged clam.

However, Wizard Wight's nature was Fair, and Wizard Cromarty's nature Foul; and throughout their youth, they scrapped and fought one another like sea-scorpions, battling over who should inherit the Great Castle's Weather Lore, and with it, the secrets of making the Weather.

Later on, they fought over who should marry the beautiful Gaia Celeste, whose job it was to encircle the planet and control its balance.

Eventually, poor Gaia Celeste, tired of all their bickering, left them both – taking the Weather Tome with her, which contained all the Weather Lore within.

She reasoned that without this book - or herself - the bickering would cease.

But it came to pass, that an unfortunate accident occurred as Gaia Celeste flew away: the heavy book slipped from her grasp and hurtled down to Earth, to land somewhere over Europe.

No-one has seen it since."

'I wonder who's got it now, Grandpa,' she'd say, drowsily as she fell asleep.

'I wonder,' was always his reply.

But now the Tome seemed to be getting heavier and heavier against her knees, and she was so tired with all the sadness of the day, that she shut it with a clunk.

Tomorrow she'd hide it in her backpack to give to Mr Allbright during the Open Day at The Weather Exhibition.

She was about to put the book safely under her pillow … when there, out-side her window, pressing its beak sideways against the glass, attempting to peer through … she thought she saw the same sooty bird she'd rescued, drenched in the pouring rain, but with the raindrops bouncing off its feathers from their chimney soot.

'Perhaps it's come to thank me,' she thought, as she fell soundly asleep.

However, her dreams, when they came that night, troubled her: strange uneasy wafts of weather tumbled her into space, and those weather-creatures in her Grandpa's bedtime story tried to pluck at her clothes - and the sea bird, squinting in at her through the window, spoke to her in angry squarks.

She awoke, hot and sweating, and tried remembering the days when she used to think it was the Shipping Forecast people like Faeroes, Fastnet and Finisterre who made the weather for them every day –

… 'and they brought us so much more of the kind of weather I loved - before all this year's windiness and storms.

I know, I'll ask my best friend, to come with me to the 'Weather Exhibition' tomorrow', she thought, sleepily.

'Raine won't mind coming along with me at all.'

This decided, Wendy drifted off, dreaming of the way the weather arrived in so many exciting variations: lovely changes of light; different rains; clever mixtures of sky and cloud. It was a bit like an orchestra,' she thought, 're-peating harmony after harmony.

… and maybe Grandpa's spirit is up there with them as well. Somewhere high up in the sky, mingling with all the stars in the firmament.

She hoped it was.

Chapter 2
Heligoland Hall

...... Viking, Cromarty, Malin, Hebrides, German Bight ...
.... gale-force winds north to north-east,
.... reaching force 10 to storm force 13 in Faeroes later.
.... visibility low ...
.... with continuous rain
.... the outlook poor in all areas

In the middle of the Irish Sea ... hovering somewhere between Latitude 4 and 5 degrees West, and Longitude 53 and 54 North, an ancient castle hovered uncertainly inside an area of extremely Low Pressure.

Like a huge whale rearing out of the sea glistening with sea-slime, the castle appeared to rise sheer from the water.

Winds howled against its ramparts; sea-spray hurled itself onto the battlements only to fall back foaming to the shore. Barnacles clung desperately to its slippery sides, and lower down between the rocks where darkness made itself at home, small crabs scurried to and fro, finding cracks to creep into and hide.

Around its shores, forgotten wrecks lurched and swayed in the gales, and over its four turrets, heavily-laden clouds furled and unfurled beneath a sky wracked with thunder and tortured with lightning.

Up above the castle, Foul Weather-Birds shrieked and cawed in the unsettling atmosphere, as they dodged the lightning-bolts.

SHAG

STORMY PETREL

SKUA

CORMORANT

GULL

FOUL WEATHER BIRDS

RAZORBILL

The castle was named Heligoland Hall.

Where the Isobars thickened towards the centre of the Depression, the heart of the Low was located directly above the chimneypots of the Kitchen.

Here, forming the lowest pressure of all, jets of black smoke shot vertically into an area of calm to fuse with the storm clouds above.

These were produced by Lundy, the Cook, preparing Devilled Crabs on Toast – German Bight's favourite meal: a just reward for the stupendous announcement he promised to make during Supper that night.

Earlier on, Lundy had trawled, from below the castle, a netful of the small unfortunate crabs, now burning in an acrid gravy of sea-mustard for this meal.

Lundy rubbed her hands on her apron, caressing the surface of her most prized possession – her Kitchen table. This had been 'obtained' by Hebrides the Black Witch from various outlandish wreckings. Fashioned from no fewer than six captain's tables, it had been welded together with fish glue and sailor's rope by Viking, Lundy's lover … that is … he

LUNDY: the Castle Cook

wasn't exactly her lover: Foul Weather-Makers are incapable of love. Nevertheless, this valiant Nordic warrior disturbed her massive heart where it thumped somewhere far beneath the folds of her apron as she moved slowly along to fetch the toasting-fork.

Lundy's Supper was almost ready. She rubbed a small clear patch into the steam of her Kitchen window and attempted to peer through, but only added grease to the steam. So instead, she threw up the window and, leaning out,

7

rested her vast bosom on its sill. All the others had worked furiously all day making their usual terrible weather. They deserved a hearty Supper before German Bight was to announce his plot.

In the gloomy courtyard, Lundy could just make out Biscay the Blustery putting the smaller Wind-Forces into their stable, after performing some kind of Advanced Dressage with them.

She heard, too, loud ringing from Viking the Thunderer's forge, as he fashioned thunderbolts on the castle anvil, ready for tomorrow's weather. The mixture of ringing metal and Foul oaths made Lundy smile. It gave colour, she thought, to that grey February day.

HEBRIDES-the-BLACK WITCH:
lightning, wrecking & fog

Another noise behind her – the sound of high-heeled boots kicking open the kitchen door - made her spin round. Framed for an instant as a jagged outline in the doorframe, Hebrides the Black Witch burst in, dressed in full wrecking gear, cruel eyes flashing like a light-house lamp. In her hands she cradled booty from her wrecks, dumping this down to steam beside the Cook's roaring hearth.

'I waited 'til all the boats came out, Lundy, then, once Viking threw out his storm, I had a field day! Three ships got wrecked.'

Out of her steaming heap of wreckage jumped a large furious toad. 'Oh yes! I rescued 'Toad' to be a present for our Castle Genius, German Bight.'

'Well, why don't you go and givit'im, Hebrides… though why a toad might

8

be hiding amongst the wreckage hell only knows. And while you're at it, sound the Foghorn for Supper's Ready. And tell GB we're all waiting on Tender Hooks for this great idea he's to announce tonight.'

German Bight had shut himself in his Study, where he'd spent the last few days working on the plot he would be presenting.

A salty capstan found floating on the Irish Sea had been captured, to be his desk, and on this, the only light - a guttering hurricane lamp (disapproving of the new whale-blubber diet it had been given) - spat rays of light into the gloom. German Bight, over-heating to finalize his idea before announcing it, had needed constantly to cool himself with his favourite Vichy water.

GERMAN BIGHT: Castle Genius, synoptic charts

'My Brilliant Bight,' cried Hebrides, bursting in.

'Ah, Hebrides, my plans all ready, all arranged.'

'I've rescued a present for you.' She placed Toad carefully to act as a paper-weight onto a pile of Weather-maps on his desk, settling it with a well-aimed spark from her fingers. Then giving a kick to his great globe of the world so it spun giddily, muddling land with sea, the Black Witch dragged him to his feet and danced him round his Study beneath all the synoptic Weather-charts pinned to the walls.

'Now you're ready, I can sound the Foghorn for Supper. Come along.' She grabbed his hand and pulled him after her, leaving behind them the globe,

9

grinding to a rusty halt.

They entered the Dining Hall arm in arm just as a special Grace was being said by Biscay, wearing one of her Weather-map headscarves, embroidered in her own Foul stitch-craft. The castle inhabitants were standing patiently behind their chairs waiting for their arrival.

Biscay's Grace

Thank you for the grand upheaval
Made from all that's bad and evil;
Deep depressions, centred Low
Several feet of freezing snow,
Gale-force winds that moan and howl
Round about the castle Foul,
Lightning, thunderbolts and rain
With a whirling weather-vane.
May our days be icy cold,
As in glacial Days of old.

May the weather over Britain
Be the worst that ever hit'em.
Captain Humber, their ancient Leader, then signalled them to sit down to crunch their crabs. To his left, sat the Castle Genius, German Bight; to his right, Malin the Bad. Next to Malin, Hebrides the Black Witch had to to put up with Sole the Doleful opposite, who continually wrung her hands and wept into her soup-

HUMBER: Captain of the Castle; outsize hailstones & snow

10

making it very salty.

Then came Biscay the Blustery, smiling. Her new Grace, she thought, had gone down quite well.

At the end of the table Viking the Thunderer presided. (He needed the extra space for his helmet with its sharply-pointed Nordic horns).

BISCAY-the-BLUSTERY
Wind

Guarding her Kitchen, the eighth member of the castle stood listening to their groans of delight, her hands crossed over her bosom, her ladle clutched frantically to her belt. Nodding with satisfaction, Lundy pressed her fat greasy hands together and made her way back to her domain.

Lundy never ate with them, preferring, as part of her pleasure, to watch how her victims attacked her food.

Besides, she was far too big for any conceivable chair.

'Well, everyone,' announced Captain Humber, 'it is exactly one year ago that Shannon, my beloved wife, was cruelly evaporated by that Fair Weather-Maker, Finisterre, who crashed into her mid-ocean. And we've retaliated with exactly a year's abysmal weather, which has totally subdued the Fair Weather-Makers at Beaufort Castle. So, now we've become so powerful, what comes next? Well, German Bight, what's this new idea of yours?'

German Bight jumped quickly to his feet. Composing himself first by smoothing his sea-jelled hair and setting his monocle on his handsome aquiline face, he announced:

11

'I'm embarking on an entirely new idea for our weather. Something I've been plotting in my Study now for days.'

VIKING-
the-
THUNDERER:
thunder & thunderbolts

The Hall grew expectant and still; voices simmered to silence. 'Continue, Bight. I'm keenly interested.' 'Yesterday, one of my spies - my favourite Stormy Petrel - flew back to inform me … that Wizard Cromarty's great Weather Tome has come to light again. Captain Humber jumped to his feet. 'Our great Weather Tome that used to be here at Heligland so long ago!

Continue, Bight. This is great news indeed - I thought it was lost forever!' 'Well, today, I can announce to you all that, once my plot is successful, the Tome will be recovered, and will be here, in this castle, laid down before you on this very table … by tomorrow evening. I think the Cabalistic Signs inside this Tome could provide us with a way to form a modern Equation which could change the whole weather pattern over Britain forever. Yes, what I'm talking about is Foul Weather Forever. Just imagine it: Ireland could eventually be Tundra; Wales, a Frigid Zone … rain pouring everlastingly over Scotland ...'

'Foul weather forever', Sole said, bursting into tears of rain and soaking her napkin.

'Foul Weather Forever! Foul Weather Forever!' they chanted.

12

Next to him, Malin the Bad heard their Captain mumbling something about making Bight Second-in-Command. Malin knew Captain Humber was getting too old now to be their Leader; that various parts of him had already started to evaporate. Malin knew he was thinking of naming a successor... and with this in mind, would announce a Second-in-Command very soon.

But with this clever idea of his, Bight was threatening his own possible promotion to that position. He froze hard with hatred.

'But in order for my plan to succeed, there's to be no Foul weather made at all tomorrow, and any already made today will have to be stored. This is vital for my plot to succeed ... You see it's An Earthly Matter that needs performing.'

'An Earthly Matter?' queried Biscay.

'Yes – it will mean making a hazardous journey down on the ground without being seen by any Earthling.

'A preposterous idea,' echoed Malin.

'And no weather to be made at all tomorrow!' snorted Viking.

Captain Humber arose and banged his soup-spoon on the table. 'Then there will be no weather manufactured tomorrow. Not even one tiny shower. Is that understood? Blue skies will be allowed overhead. And we wish our brave German Bight well on this dangerous undertaking of his.'

The Foul Weather-Makers left the table sulking. Viking went off to grind

13

and sharpen his thunderbolts; Biscay began stitching a new Weather-Forecast headscarf; Hebrides polished her black thigh-length boots … and Captain Humber, himself, absentmindedly forgot to store in the Heligoland Freezer

SOLE-the-DOLEFUL:
Rain

the hailstones he'd carved so painstakingly all day – so, once again, they melted away, leaving him a pool of water for all his pains.

Poor, dismal Sole, whose raining she found so hard to control, went up to weep some rain-drops privately in her room.

(Sole's room was a place of sheer delight: leaking gutters spluttered steadily, ferns clung to the drainpipe, bladderwrack seaweed littered the floor.

Due to an unattended aperture in the main chimney, blue mustard smoke and Kitchen steam, left over from the Devilled Crabs, wafted into her room, curling over the edges of wilting posters, which portrayed different types of rain, and had been impaled on the walls with rusty drawing-pins.)

Taking several gulps from her vat of boiling cough mixture, to which she was addicted, Sole made her way among her Post-it messages which lay in damp drifts entangled with the bladder-wrack, and went to sulk on her bed, trying to staunch her weeping eye-lids so they would shut and allow her to get some sleep.

Chapter 3
Wendy Gets Blown Away

Down on Earth, Wendy was about to leave her house, dressed in her usual warm clothes, plus mac and clutching an umbrella. She had her Grandpa's green Tome wrapped safely inside her backpack to give to Mr Allbright as her Grandpa had instructed…

But then, a quite extraordinary thing occurred: the sky suddenly turned a perfect blue. The temperature climbed quickly, the sun blazed down … quite hot for a February day.

Sometime later, Wendy re-emerged, wearing just a T-shirt and jeans, with the Tome still safe in her backpack.

Wendy's friend, Raine, soon joined her. She'd changed her clothes as well. Raine was pleased to accompany Wendy to the Weather Exhibition, though she wasn't quite as interested in the weather as Wendy, but was happy enough to chat about it as they went along.

'Mr Allbright', she said, 'mentioned absolutely nothing about today's heat-wave in the news. He'd predicted stormy weather and "exceptionally cold temperatures for the time of year" – as usual.'

The Exhibition was packed when they arrived. Everybody from the city had ventured outside, amazed at the change in the weather. Many were visiting the Exhibition, blinking through strong sunlight.

Wendy had told Raine about giving Mr Allbright the large book she carried in her backpack.

However, they couldn't get anywhere near the new Chief Weather-Man. Some were pestering him for his autograph, others haranguing him over why his weather predictions for today had been so Entirely Wrong.

'I know, let's go up that spiral staircase, Raine. Let's look at all the wind machines and measuring devices they said they've put out on the roof for us to look at today,' Wendy suggested.

'OK', Raine agreed; 'and you can give Mr Allbright your book later on.'

Wendy was already climbing swiftly ahead of Raine … because she found herself being strongly drawn upwards, as if a magnet was pulling … making her follow some strange humming noises made by all the weather machines.

The tour hadn't reached the roof yet. Nobody else was around.

Raine was the only witness to what happened next.

Why, if it was fine with hardly any breeze at all, were the Anemometers whirling round faster and faster?

Why were the Barographs scratching out feverish measures of pressure onto cylinders with a twitching, urgent needle?

Why was a troubled Wind-sock billowing and straining on its pole?

Looking westwards, Wendy caught sight of a thin funnel of grey cloud spinning furiously fast out of a completely blue sky.

And before she could even turn to run back, its pointed end had reached the Exeter Met Office roof, whirling her around, trying to suck the backpack away from her.

But Wendy swung it in front of her, so she could clutch it close with both arms.

'Raine!' she screamed, 'Help!' as the funnel whisked both her and her backpack clean off the roof and up into the void.

She didn't even hear the terrified shriek from Raine, when she saw her friend disappear.

When Raine was given the 'Observer's Book Of Weather' to look through, she pointed to a tornado and said,

'Yes, that's exactly what it was that snatched Wendy away.'

Wendy was unable to recall much of her journey inside the whirling wind. She remembered being stretched out like a piece of chewing gum until she became a cloud; then spun round and round like a weather-device measuring the wind.

Later on, her temperature dropped severely as she was drawn sideways and enveloped in an icy blanket of mist, which pressed slowly into her brain, until darkness blotted her out.

Chapter 4
Celebration Pie

German Bight was slumped down exhausted in his study.

The small Tornado - (normally the work of Biscay the Blustery), had been difficult for him to create – especially as it needed to be strong enough to carry both Tome and Earthling back to Heligoland Hall.

Bringing that Earthling back as well, of course, had been a huge mistake. But Bight had been unable to prise the huge book away from her. He'd thrown the Earthling into the dungeon ... to deal with later. Her backpack was waiting in front of him now, lying on his Capstan desk. But before tackling it, he needed to get some air.

Walking the castle ramparts in order to work up enough energy to engage with such an important and powerful book, he heard, from the stables, some of Biscay's little Wind-Forces whimpering and whining among themselves, very choppy and nervous after being kept inside for the whole day. He'd be pleased to see everybody back making their usual Foul weather the following morning. He also hoped he'd be rewarded for this ingenious whirlwind-capture of Cromarty's Tome by being made Second-in-Command ... for whoever was made Second, would soon become First.

With his energy restored, German Bight entered his Study, locking it tight behind him. Then ready to work he saw that Toad was sitting on the backpack with a heavy stillness, guarding it as he'd requested.

Bight brushed the creature aside, then wrenched the huge captured book out ... and noticed that the cover, when he touched it, turned from a boring green to a far more satisfying black.

Gloating over his prize, German Bight set to, poring over page after page of its strange symbols and spells.

And as he did so, he felt power flowing into him from every page.

'Now, if I can only just work up some kind of Equation from all these Cabalistic signs ...'

All night long German Bight worked, arranging possible combinations of the ancient signs, scribbling away until he had all his pencils worn down to the place where it says 2b, and carried several green biro smudges around his lips, making him look alarmingly demonic.

Wendy moaned as she came round, awoken eventually by the crashing of waves outside.

'Where am I?' she cried … except her voice came out all dim and shadowy.

She got unsteadily to her feet, shivering with fear.

To her amazement, she appeared to weigh hardly anything at all. 'My clothes! – They're falling off me!'

She pulled up her jeans, which had landed in a pile at her feet, and tied them tightly back with a long length of seaweed she found on the floor nearby.

That was when she discovered she was no longer the solidly-muscled girl she'd once been; but stretched and thinned into a peculiar wispy thing – 'rather like one of those creatures I saw in my dreams,' she thought. 'But this isn't a dream … it feels real…. and I feel quite … what was the word Grandpa often used Insubstantial… that's it. I feel quite Insubstantial.'

At her mention of Grandpa, everything flooded back. She looked around wildly for the backpack, which carried his precious Tome. It wasn't there anymore …

'Oh No! Grandpa made me promise to be its Guardian! And I've let him down already and lost it!'

Wendy was suddenly really frightened. She seemed to be trapped in a horrid damp dungeon, smelling of ozone like the sea. She gulped … tried to cry; but the tears trickling down her cheeks felt more like raindrops and only made her T-shirt damper.

So she went over to peer through a small grille, set into the wall, to see why waves were pounding her dungeon-side.

Wendy gasped at the scene.

Suspended there in the atmosphere outside, was a giant spiral of concentric rings composed of fat bands of filmy vapour … 'just like the isobars on a weather map. How very odd.'

A flurry of snowflakes drifted past her grille, and Wendy was startled to find she could actually see the intricate geometric designs that every dancing flake made. 'How beautiful! I've always wanted that – to be able to see snowflake patterns without having a microscope. It almost feels as if I'm part of the weather itself.'

For some time she stood watching transfixed, puzzled - and entranced. She clutched at a pretty snowflake through the bars – but it melted almost immediately in her grasp, the pattern dissolving as disappointingly fast.

Could anyone be outside to rescue her?

'Help! Help!' she called through the iron bars. Her voice came out so thinly. She called louder.

To her delight, her favourite sea bird – a Kittiwake - flew down, calling back at her with the same sound its name made: 'Kittiwake! Kittiwake!'

'Help me, Kittiwake. I've been imprisoned!' she cried … uselessly … knowing sea birds couldn't speak.

But the Kittiwake answered. 'Kittiwake! Kittiwake! I saw you arriving. I followed to investigate. Kittiwake! Kittiwake! I'll get help if I can … but it's unsafe for me here … in enemy waters. I was sent here from the Fair Weather-Makers at Beaufort Castle to see why the weather was suddenly so fine yesterday.'

And the sea-bird flew bravely away.

*

Inside the Heligoland Kitchen, Lundy was back at work like the rest of the inhabitants of Heligoland Hall.

She was in the process of creating a Celebration Meal to applaud German Bight's success.

Moving past huge tubs of sea-salt; extractors for squeezing the juice from sea-slugs before they went into the aspic; pestles to crush and grind molluscs; skewers for trussing sea birds, she came at last to her larder. There she rested her finger on the surface of a magnificent Barnacle Jelly, setting steadily for the dessert … and gave a cry of dismay …

'But it's not setting!' Lundy glared at her handiwork. 'I can't produce a failure - not for a Celebration Dessert!'

Angrily, she tipped in half a bottle of aga-aga, her special seaweed gelatine, to encourage her pudding to harden. But this only made it cloudy. (And Lundy never produced a culinary failure. Her Flounder Soup was unrivalled, her Cormorant Puddings unbeatable and guaranteed to make everyone feel very ill. Hers was a model kitchen, full of flavours and delights; and everything she cooked in it was served with extremely bad taste and appreciated by all).

And therein lay Lundy's powers, for whenever she thought the Foul Weather-Makers were slacking, she merely threw the contents of her pans onto the ramparts for the Foul Sea-Birds to eat … or occasionally straight into the Irish Sea … to fatten her crabs and whelks which stalked the bottom. After moans of hunger and a few ungracious threats, the Foul Force would set to work again … so, in a way, Lundy could be said to control the workings of the whole castle from her Kitchen.

Lundy searched the ceiling-hooks for a fat piece of whale-blubber to make her pastry. Choosing one that looked interesting, she hauled it down with her boat-hook.

Some juicy slices of lard were soon carved off and chopped into pieces on the marble slab. And before long, with sleeves wedged well above her elbows and arms plunged deep inside the mixing-bowl, Lundy pounded away at the flour and blubber, working out her resentment of the unsetting Barnacle Jelly into the pastry … until tears forced their way from her eyes, over-flavouring the mixture, and making it go sticky.

Once kneaded together, this dough seemed to heave itself up from the bowl into the cook's floured hands, and suffer itself to be pummelled. Out of this, Lundy rolled one large blanket to line an outsize dish, another to be its crust on top.

The clatter of high-heeled boots brought Hebrides the Black Witch into the Kitchen - this time with a present for Lundy.

'I was walking round our battlements just now, Lundy, when suddenly, I noticed a Fair Weather-Bird - undoubtedly an enemy spy - winging fast away. So, pointing one of my long, bony fingers at it, with one crackle I electrified the poor creature, just enough to grab it by its feet.'

Hebrides held out her gift. 'Here, Lundy, this 'free-range' present is for you.'

And she pressed the poor fluttering Kittiwake into Lundy's floured hands ... 'Thanks, Hebrides. How kind. Just what I wanted for my Pie.'

The gift cheered Lundy considerably and, on accepting the bird, she tentatively placed a thumb on its head to steady it, leaving behind a floured thumb-print as a kind of blessing.

Then, on an impulse, she added, 'I was going to use UFO's (Unidentified Flying Objects) from the Heligoland Freezer, but, as it's a special day, we'll have fresh to go with this Kittiwake. More Fair Weather-Birds'll do.'

Seizing an implement of a torturous nature from the racks, Lundy marched towards a wire cage swinging from a hook above the Kitchen window. 'Come 'ere my little darlins' she threatened the squawking imprisoned birds, going away with half a dozen Godwits by their feet. 'In you all go.'

The Kittiwake was pushed towards the furthest end of the pie, allowing the Godwits to remain at the nearside of the pie-chimney.

Next, Lundy drew the great pastry-lid over their heads, and with her large thumb, pressed around the edge of the crust to join the upper and lower pastries together, leaving her thumb-print again as a pretty pattern all the way around.

Then, as an afterthought, she added, through the air-vent of the pie-chimney, a pinch of Conger Curry-powder obtained from the solid row of bottles before her, each plugged with a cork found floating on the Irish Sea, and,

'There now!' she sighed.

Her pie was complete.

But, while Lundy and Hebrides were discussing the Plot that German Bight was to reveal that evening, inside the pie-crust the fat Kittiwake came round. Now fully awake, and judging from the cook's voice that she was chatting to somebody a suitable distance away, it started to peck around the chimney's air-vent on its side of the pie.

Suddenly Hebrides screamed as an apparition arose from the pie – with sticky bits of pastry and Conger Curry-powder dropping off its wings. It soared around the room looking for an exit.

'Quick! Shut the door, Hebrides!' yelled Lundy, chasing the pastry-bird down the length of her table. 'Watch out! Scum and fish-bones! Here it comes!'

The Kittiwake, frantic and fearful, darted about, banking violently to avoid the drying fish hanging from the rafters. But Lundy twirled dramatically and, after the third fly-past, was able to give it an accurate swipe with her ladle, knocking it senseless in flight, sending it hurtling into the larder.

The Kittiwake landed straight into the Barnacle Jelly, setting in time for supper. Obligingly, the opaque pudding gulped it down, levelled over and, in the shock-waves, decided to set.

Hebrides and Lundy searched the larder from top to bottom, but were unable to find the Kittiwake.

Eventually, they gave up; time was running out. To make up for its loss, Lundy grasped a fat curlew from the wire cage. Stuffing this replacement through the enlarged pie-vent, she patched the crust as best she could - and placed the nuisance in the oven before there was any more nonsense.

Chapter 5
German Bight's Plot

When the Foghorn sounded for his Celebration Meal, German Bight had only got a small way along with a possible Equation. He was exasperated – knowing he'd need much more help if he were to get any further forming one.

In the Dining Hall, the members of Heligoland sat staring at the table, which seemed to be laid with an inordinate amount of cutlery. An impressive dessert, scattered with bright red starfish gently quivering over its surface, stood on the sideboard.

German Bight's announcement was to be made directly the meal was over. He, himself, sat proprietorially on the weighty volume by Johann Heinrich Lambert, which he'd brought up from his dungeon Study to show them all. Its thickness caused him to be four inches taller on his chair.

'They're eating at a rattling pace,' Lundy remarked. 'Obviously they're dying to hear how Bight's got on.'

So she cleared away their soup plates fast, then grabbed several fish kettles from her Kitchen fire, where they bubbled and frothed onto the flames below as if they could bear their contents no longer. So she relieved them of their agonized boiling, drained their remains through a pair of Viking's old pyjama bottoms, and served this fish course next door.

Lundy, now steeped in the very heart of her cooking, opened the oven door: 'Oh Horrors! Dump me Downwards! My pie's not done. What'll I do? All that nonsense with the Kittiwake has cut down badly on its cooking time. I'd best giv'em an extra course to fill the gap.'

She ran trembling hands along 'Disgusting Degustation' and 'Uncouth Cookery,' coming to rest on 'Great Foul Dishes of the World.'

Searching for 'Omelette Deluxe', she thought piercingly of the snobbish Finisterre who was Cordon Bleu Cook for the Fair Weather-Makers at Beaufort Castle, and how rumour had it that her pompous breakfast menus stated: 'Eggs cooked in their own jackets' – when everyone knew she meant an ordinary hard-boiled egg.

'An egg is an egg is an egg,' Lundy sang, cracking open one hundred and fifty Guillemots, four Puffins and one addled Fulmer's egg for flavour;

worried her Omelette Deluxe for a moment over the flames, and served it smartly next door.

'Well, Bight, let's hear how you've got on, then.' Captain Humber ordered. 'It looks like nobody can wait a moment longer.'

German Bight (who'd nervously drunk more than necessary) rose to his feet. Clearing a space in front, he placed the Tome on the table.

'By Thor and Thunder, Bight, You're a Genius.' Humber was filled with glee. 'You have returned our long-lost Weather-book. Excellent. Excellent. Carry on. Carry on.'

They all crowded round, staring at its strange old-fashioned symbols. But no-one could make anything of them.

'As you know, modern signs, similar to these, are used by me every day, plotted when I draw up our daily Synoptic Weather-Charts, and carried out accordingly when our weather is made.'

'Yes, yes, we all know that,' said Malin, snidely. 'Get on with it, Bight.'

German Bight frowned at his rival. 'Well, I've discovered that if some of these ancient but potent symbols were worked together in a specific way, they'd be powerful enough for us to easily win a Weather War against the Fair Weather-Makers, and get rid of our opponents completely... It will be just what they deserve for one of them evaporating our dear Queen, Shannon.'

'War? And why not?' applauded Biscay. 'It's definitely the next step after our whole year of Foul Weather. I'll start training a Foul Feathered Force if you like. Straight away.'

'Splendid idea,' bellowed Viking.

Sole wriggled uncomfortably on her chair. But Malin scowled at German Bight – though no one was aware of Malin's scowl, for it was frozen beneath his normal expression.

Hebrides' eyes, however, flamed with fervour. 'My brilliant, brilliant Bight!'

Humber saw that their excitement was causing a dangerous atmospheric pressure to rise. He called Lundy in and asked her to let out a small Snow-storm of his own making from the Heligoland Freezer to cool the Dining Hall down.

Before long, pretty flakes were dancing over their heads, and German Bight proceeded with explaining his plan.

24

'You see, now that Britain has been fully-subjected to a complete year of our continual Foul Weather - well, the time has come I think, to take this a little further. But the next step - this Weather War - can only be waged once a strong enough Equation is formed from this Tome - then there's nothing can stop us...'

'Yes, Bight'll likely be our Second-in-Command after this proposal,' Captain Humber thought. 'I like a man who shows initiative,' he mumbled aloud.

Malin's blood turned from blue to green with envy. But his smoothly-chiselled features were unable to flinch, for the stuff that was his blood gave no warmth to his face at all, and his cold heart could scarcely pump it round. He tried to think of reasons why Bight would be incapable of carrying out this great scheme.

'Wasn't it only last week, Bight, that you built up an immense cloud-system ... wind arrows whizzing everywhere; then, too impatient, you let the air pressure get completely out of control. Sure enough, the whole structure suffered an Inversion; collapsed before your very eyes. It was ME had to sort out the mess, while YOU went off in a huff. And you say an Equation CAN be formed. But I don't believe you can do it – not even with Hebrides' help.'

'I CAN! Listen, won't you.' German Bight snapped at Malin's taunting. He'd thought of a sudden ingenious idea ... a way he could get out of this sticky situation ... Why not make the captured Earthling part of his plan?

'The book's Guardian is waiting in the Dungeon,' he announced.

'By the North Wind itself! An Earthling here to help?' shouted Viking.

'Yes! My Stormy Petrel spied through the window of her room on Earth. It saw her pouring over the Tome with avid interest, far into the night. She'll know everything about these Cabalistic symbols, I assure you.'

Malin had not thought that his rival would come up with such a daring ploy. His temperature plummeted with jealously, causing his trousers to freeze to his chair.

Lundy, seeing Malin's defeat from the Kitchen door, chuckled. She loved to see that frigid man upset; he had no sense of humour, always complained if his porridge was more than nine days old. Also, he had the annoying habit of letting his tea get quite cold before he would drink it, lest its sudden heat would break a blood vessel. I ask you!'

'Sole, go and fetch this Earthling for us, then', Humber ordered. 'She'll be less intimidated by you. Say something like … it's … it's to celebrate her arrival.'

'Everyone picks on me. S'not fair', muttered Sole. But she did as she was bid, going peevishly; leaving a long slime-trail behind her as she went.

'Oh, by the way, Bight, was any other Earthling witness to your clever capture of their kind?' asked Humber.' It would be useful to know.'

'Only her friend, Rainy, saw her disappear. I heard the Earthling calling out to her: "Help! Rainy. Help!"'

'And will this Rainy person cause trouble? I hope not; we do not show ourselves to Earthlings if we can help it.'

While the Earthling was being fetched, Lundy carefully lifted her Celebration Pie from the oven and put the skewer through into the Godwits.

'There are no squeaks so it must be done,' she thought.

Everyone clapped in delight as this course was served. The pastry was perfectly undercooked and fell in their stomachs like stones. They all had the feeling now that everything would be all right.

Wendy heard a loud sneeze outside her dungeon. Then a key was turned and the door pushed open on rusty hinges.

A dismal creature slid inside.

Wendy had never seen anything quite so ghastly: its red nose dripped continually like a leaking tap, long dank hair looked as if it had never been brushed, moistly-hanging clothes as if they'd never been ironed. And Wendy couldn't help shuddering as Sole slimed towards her and enclosed Wendy's hand in her wet one.   Speechless with dismay, Wendy allowed herself to be slid into lunch. What else could she do?

She was even more terrified as she entered the Dining Hall, so kept her eyes lowered. They seated her next to Sole, but she soon spotted what must be her Grandfather's Tome on the table, and a handsome man, (though rather flushed), looking very eager and important, had one hand resting on its cover. This, she noticed, had turned an oily-looking black - instead of the nice green it had been for her. Did that mean the Tome changed its appearance depending on who was in charge of it she wondered? How magical it must be.

Her captors had already started on their meal, but now they paused to stare in amazement at the strange Mortal in her loose apparel, held up by a sea-weed strand.

No-one had ever visited Heligoland Hall before.

They waited and watched while the Earthling tasted some of their Foul Soup before they questioned her.

Wendy gazed down at her bowl. Strange ingredients seemed to be wandering around in the soup. But she was rather hungry and it wasn't so bad once you got going. The thin layer of tar at the bottom even strengthened her a little.

Captain Humber rose with glass in hand.

'Quiet, please,' he ordered the inhabitants, who were already silent.

'I'd like to Toast our special guest with some of Hebrides' plankton wine. Everyone, raise your glasses please.'

Lundy had come from the Kitchen to see what was going on, and joined them in the Toast.

Wendy felt more comfortable: they were treating her as an honoured guest now. So, politely, she took a sip of the green stuff from her own glass. It surprised her – it was rather tasty, and gave her a little more courage.

'What's your name, dear?'

'Wendy', she answered.

'Windy - an excellent name.'

'Hear. Hear,' cried Biscay, her headscarf folding into pleats. 'Jolly good Show!'

They allowed the Earthling more time to enjoy her portion of Celebration Pie; but Wendy soon found far too many feathers and beaks that had to be spat out after every mouthful. So, as she had been taught, she placed her knife and fork in the finishing position on her plate.

'Well, then, Windy, can you help us form an Equation with your great book of Cabalistic Signs?'

Only now did Wendy understand. So that's why they'd got her here. At once, all the claws, feathers and beaks she'd not been able to spit out, began racing around in her stomach.

'Oh no! Only my Grandfather could understand them,' she replied, 'but he never told anyone else about them. He said they were "far too dangerous."'

27

Everyone groaned with disappointment

… Except Malin, who was pleased that his rival's big scheme had turn out a flop.

'So, Bight … think you can form an Equation now on your own, do you?'

German Bight sat down, crestfallen. Malin was right: in one cruel blow, his ingenious plot had been blown sky high, or sunk as surely as if it had been one of Hebrides' own wrecks.

And Malin took full advantage. He rose to his feet, leaving much of his frozen trouser-seat stuck to the chair.

Rigid with hate, he scraped his fork across a plate with an unbearable noise. Then he fixed the table with such a hideous stare that a chill passed through them, making them grow hushed and afraid. When Malin was like this, the sound of his voice made you shiver; one glance from his eyes could freeze you to the spot.

'This Guardian has proved useless. She will have to be evaporated immediately … as for Bight …'

Wendy was horrified at what they were going to do with her. She looked round sharply, appealing for help.

But no one seemed to be paying attention to her any more. It was as if they'd already evaporated her from their minds.

She stared hopelessly at a weird display of stuffed sardines, anchovies and prawns on the mantelpiece, as if asking for their help. Next, her eyes rested on a more interesting picture made from an arrangement in limpets and whelks, which she recognized as being Botticelli's 'Venus rushing into shore on her sea-shell', all stuck to a piece of driftwood with some sticky stuff … and signed 'Hebrides'. That was no comfort to her either; so she began crying gently into the remains of her Celebration Pie.

But Lundy, who'd always wanted a child of her own, felt sorry for the Earthling. Fetching her Barnacle Jelly dessert from the sideboard, she placed its scarlet presence near to the weeping Earthling to please her.

Hebrides was thoroughly dismayed. Her German Bight was in disgrace.

'I could try to form an equation with Bight if you wish,' she offered. 'I like the idea of a Weather War against the Fair Weather-Makers. Think of it, if we won, I'd be able to wreck as often as I liked. I also love the idea of their Beaufort Castle being blown to bits … then, just imagine, Lundy, you'd be able to cook all those Fair Weather-Birds in your pies – one after another…'

'SQUARK!'

Suddenly, there was an almighty bulging of the dessert as an indignant Fair Weather-Bird wobbled free of the Barnacle Jelly and shot up from the table.

Lundy grabbed the ladle from her belt. 'The wretch! So that's where it's been hiding! This time I'll fetch it one!'

'Catch it, Lundy, Catch it!' everyone screamed.

But this time, Kittiwake was wise to her moves, and knew what it had to do. With a wild cry, it executed a magnificent U-dive, swooped up the chimney, and was soon out of sight and into the air.

Viking flung his trident into the grate; Sole burst into sobs, flooding the Dining Hall floor. German Bight, with one leap, dashed open a window and screamed for the Foul Weather-Birds.

Within minutes a black flock of Stormy Petrels flew over; then Cormorants, Shags, Razorbills and the Great Black-backed Gulls all came hurtling through the air to obey his command.

'Fly off after that Kittiwake! You can't miss it. It's a Fair Weather Spy. It'll be making straight towards Beaufort Castle to warn them of our intended War.'

But the Kittiwake had accumulated such a thick layer of sticky black soot on its journey up the chimney that, when it emerged from the pot, it looked like all the other Foul Weather-Birds flying outwards in pursuit.

Lundy was in disgrace. What was a Fair Weather-Bird doing in the dessert? With this one culinary mistake, the cook had probably given their whole plot away.

Lundy made a fast exit into her Kitchen, and curled up inside her largest pan where she knew she'd be safe, while the useless Earthling was thrown back once more into the dungeon.

'Til I, not anyone else, decides what will become of her,' ordered Humber.

'Now listen everyone; there's only one thing to be done: we've got to prevent the bird from reaching Beaufort Castle to warn them. There's to be a gigantic storm. Viking, give it everything you've got; Hebrides, throw out lightning; Sole, create a rain-storm; Biscay, your strongest winds. Fast as you can!'

Viking and Hebrides worked side by side. Throughout the night, their devastating weather smashed the skies to a pulp. Biscay's Force 12 wind ripped apart the Heligoland Flag (which now read briefly: 'HEL'). Great ships, which had set sail in the sudden calm weather the day before, ran helpless before colossal waves; both Fair and Foul Weather-Birds were dashed to death onto cliffs, or pulled beneath the waves.

The people of Britain put sand-bags out before hiding inside their homes having barred their doors and windows.

The storm was a resounding success. For, just after dawn, Heligoland Hall received three Greater black-backed Gulls flying in over the horizon on beating wings, bearing the tidings it longed to hear:

'We've found her! We've found her!' they chorused.

'Flying barely above the waves,' said one.

'So what did we do?' said another.

'Broke one of her wings,' said the third.

'And twisted a leg,' said the second.

'And sent her tumbling down,' said the first.

'Floating downside up in the Channel.'

'Won't last more than an hour.'

'She'll sink like a stone.'

'She's as good as a goner.' They all squawked. 'Where's our reward?'

'Well done indeed, everyone,' said Captain Humber. 'Congratulations. Our secret's safe. Biscay, see that these Sea-Birds fly round to Lundy's Kitchen window to get their rewards … Oh, and tell Lundy she's forgiven … or we'll have nothing to eat for Breakfast, and everyone's both hungry and exhausted.'

Down in the Dungeon, terrified by the gigantic storm that had raged all night long, Wendy was curled tightly into a ball. Now it was morning and the Foul Weather finally over, she uncurled and sat up frozen, hungry … and with a sinking feeling of soon being evaporated - whenever that Leader decided.

Several 'other things' had crawled or slithered in through the window-bars during the night, hiding from the storm.

A small inland sea had developed in one corner of her dungeon, and these

30

Sea-Creatures lay quietly in its wetness - a flat fish flapped and flopped, a lobster lay quietly in the corner, a pile of jellyfish heaved.

For a while, Wendy sat dejectedly watching her new companions - who were probably all as frightened as she was. Then she made her way over to the grille and peered out. The sea looked choppy, but the atmosphere outside was much warmer.

She began to cry all over again, knowing that her only friend, Kittiwake, who could've gone for help, would've been pursued by a pack of horrible birds through the sky. They'd catch up with it and kill it. It'd never come back to save her.

A little later, she thought she saw through the castle gloom – but wasn't entirely sure – the same shadowy figures from the Dining-Hall glide silently from turret to turret outside, checking a torn wind-sock, reading Anemometers and attending to other strange weather business.

And she really did see some Wind-Forces blow by. They were almost transparent, and being trained by that strange lady with the Weather-map headscarf, who now held a seaweed whip in her hand. Also, the dismal one who'd taken her to the meal, drizzled past.

'Now what am I supposed to do?' She asked the Sea-Creatures.

Then suddenly, Wendy was furious: how dare these Weather-Makers treat her like this!

'I don't even know where I am. I've got to find out. There must be some way I can get back Grandpa's Tome and get away from this foul dungeon before they evaporate me? I have to escape!'

Later still, she heard her Dungeon door being unlocked; then, after a loud sneeze, the same dismal creature slid in.

'I've been asked to bring you some food Lundy's made,' the apparition stuttered nervously, wringing her hands.

She seems frightened of me, Wendy thought. What a weedy creature. So, trying to strengthen her voice, she demanded,

'Who are you all? Where am I exactly? No-one's even bothered to tell me.'

'I'm … I'm … Sole. In charge of Rain … and we're at the centre of a Deep Depression – it's always Low Pressure here. It gets me down.' And she sneezed again.

31

'Tell me properly where I am then, Sole?'

But the dismal creature was already back-sliding.

She shoved the Earthling's plate of food along the floor towards her. 'This is Hel … Heligoland Hall,' she answered in a gust of Foul air as she closed the door fast and, re-locking it, slipped away.

Wendy stared, horrified, at the plate of food Sole had brought … and her appetite left her completely when she saw her 'meal' begin to move.

(This was because Lundy's idea of a crab sandwich was to slap a live crab between two slices of bread. And by the time Sole reached the dungeons, the 'crusty slices' were tear-soaked and limp.) So Wendy allowed her sandwich to scuttle into the corner away from the other Sea-Creatures … where it became engrossed in eating its own lid.

As a reward for the resting workers, Lundy excelled herself with the most violent of Seaweed Soups for Supper. Storm-damaged Sea-kill formed the main course, dredged from the surface of the Irish Sea … 'All Free-range', she explained. As for dessert, they deserved 'A Colony of Sandlings cooked in Bird's Custard'.

Everyone clapped; they were in a Victorious Mood. And they went on clapping and jeering in all the right places when, for a special early evening entertainment, Hebrides produced one of her one-act plays.

With a few economic gestures of her long bony hands, she described a shipwreck in such a way, you felt you were at the scene itself. Hebrides played all the parts … killing off all the 'extras' first … then herself dying heroically.

As usual, she remained in a collapsed state (centre stage), entranced by her own over-acting - until Viking carried her off to her room, with the cardboard dagger still sticking out of her chest.

Then Captain Humber stood up to speak.

'Hebrides' play has given me an excellent idea. Let's create a small Depression of our own around the Castle - like a kind of theatrical curtain… a Foggy LOW, behind which, we can secretly manufacture weather for our proposed Weather War.

Meanwhile, you, German Bight, will work out an Equation from these Cabalistic signs with Hebrides.'

'Listen! Why don't we allow the Fair Weather-Makers to make all the daily weather while we do so,' offered Viking. ' They'll just think our powers are waning.'

This was an extremely good idea, and was voted in.

In the aftermath of Viking's storm, the waves were swollen and turbulent out in the Bristol Channel.

*

Under a canopy of orange sunset, the remaining clouds flew by with sharply-tattered edges, chasing across the skies like ragged witches' skirts.

Below them, way down on the metallic sea, a small black speck danced a lonely dance, resembling a buoyant cork bobbing on the waves.

Kittiwake, her head bent backwards over a broken wing, hadn't "sunk like a stone". The same greasy layer of soot that had disguised her escape from Heligoland Hall, had saved her life by keeping her afloat. It acted, too, as a warm, protective blanket to keep her softly-beating heart from freezing ... for many a long hour to come.

Part Two
Beaufort

The Cast of
WEATHER or NOT

At Beaufort Castle
THE FAIR WEATHER-MAKERS

FAEROES-the-GOOD : King of Beaufort

FAIR ISLE – Mermaiden : warm showers & blue skies

WIZARD WIGHT : hot spells and Light Effects

FASTNET : Castle Secretary; High Pressure

FISHER : weather equipment, calm weather & fishing

FORTIES – Cloud-Maker: clouds & rock pigeons

NANNY DOVER – in charge of Castle children

BEAUFORT CHILDREN – Tyne &Thames

DOGGER and BAILEY – Weather Sentinels

Fair Weather Birds
Kittiwakes, Guillemot, Gannets, Fulmars, Snow Geese, Rock Pigeons

At Sunny Intervals
a Detached Residence in the Azores

FINISTERRE-the-WHITE WITCH/FITZROY : Cordon Bleu Cook for
Beaufort Castle, and Fitzroy, her male 'other half'.
(N.B. The shipping area of Finisterre was changed to Fitzroy on 4th Feb, 2002)

Chapter 6
Beaufort Castle

High above the White Cliffs of Dover, where great white cloud-banks mass over the English Channel, one huge Cumulus cloud towered above the rest in a majestic mound, measuring nearly 5,000 feet from base to top. Developed vertically in the Perpendicular Style, this Towering Cumulus was named Beaufort Castle.

Around its ramparts billowed the weight of lavish ornament. Flying buttresses were topped with fine fluff finials. These wound upwards to support Turrets, which themselves were composed of tier upon tier of High Gothic tracery.

Here, the Fair Weather-Makers lived, producing spells of Fine Weather by clearing away grey clouds to let the Sunshine through.

Inside their castle, the cloudy magnificence continued: high-domed ceilings were braced with delicate fan-vaulting, which branched outwards in radiating ribs towards lofty lancet windows, themselves wrought with gentle wisps of cloud in Cirrus curlicues.

FAROES-the-GOOD
King of Beaufort

Today, the smell of hot-buttered toast drifted down its corridors and filtered out through the Library windows where Faeroes-the-Good, King of the Fair Weather-Makers, leaned against the sill. Blue smoke from the toast drifted about his hair and stung his pale turquoise eyes. But the gaze was fixed, the eyes unblinking. His thoughts were far away – and they experienced premonitions of danger.

'Somewhere in the atmosphere an evil force is producing an increased uneasiness around our Castle. We used to be able to dispel everything the Foul Weather-Makers flung at us – but for a whole year now, they have dominated the skies with rain, thunder, fog ...

Then yesterday, suddenly, we managed excellent Fine Weather... simply because Heligoland was making none.

I sent out Kittiwake to spy what could be happening there –But she still hasn't returned – Now I fear for her life.'

'Then throughout last night, a really massive storm, coming from Heligoland Hall crashed the sea-waves together and tore up the skies ... yet today again, we're able to make perfect weather ...

I just don't understand. Fair Isle has practically run out of 'blue' for blue skies, Fastnet, her widespread warm weather - and Forties-the-Hefty hasn't much 'fluff' left to form any of his small puffy clouds. I'd better call a Meeting during High Tea. It's all so strange ... I'm filled with such foreboding ...'

King Faeroes looked above him, as if asking advice from the ancient Greek Winds set one in each corner of his room: Notos, the South Wind, Boreas, the North Wind, Appeliotes, the East, and Zephyros, the West. Carved from stratified cloud, their faces were weathered into an interesting patina.

But the Greek Winds stared blankly back.

Even Selene the Moon Goddess, who made up the central boss, smiled down serene as ever.

'Everything's so normal, yet ...'

Faeroes sighed and went to lean over the balcony to watch with love the Castle Children playing with Nanny Dover. They'd just completed a complicated star-pattern game in singsong chanting, which echoed against the cloud-cut walls.

> *A is for Altocumulus.*
> *B is for bright blue skies,*
> *C is for Fair-Weather clouds*

... D is for Finisterre's Depressions.

Faeroes frowned again, allowing some static electricity to work up in his scalp, causing his hair to crackle. ' "D is for Finisterre's Depressions" … that wasn't in the rhyme when I was young ... Yes, Finisterre's Depressive state has got far worse. She produces Low pressure most of the time here when it should be High – She's upsetting the equilibrium of the whole Castle. How can we oppose Foul Weather with her still around? I must be strong - do something drastic. She'll have to go.

Oh dear, worrying's not good for me - or anyone else in Beaufort Castle.'

Faeroes ran lightly down the stairs that lead to the Long Gallery to search for Fair Isle, his wife.

Instead, he saw through an opened window, Fisher, perched right on the Cloud-edge, concentrating hard on a long line that reached far into the salty sea below.

He looked so contented fishing for their super, that Faeroes felt ashamed.

'What right have I to be worried when the atmosphere appears so calm today again? Making a downpour out of a raindrop maybe?'

And then, looking through another cloud window, could see Fair Isle at last.

She was sitting on a cloud-mound, knitting a new Wind-Sock, prettily-patterned with designs of ancient runes and myths in intricate Fair Isle colours.

He remembered the first time they'd met. He was young, and often dared

39

walk down on Earth, leading his Wind-Force along a deserted seashore. All at once, he caught sight of a Mermaiden sitting on a rock, combing out her hair. This was made of seaweed and looked very easy to tangle. Her body was quite exquisite: soft, smooth as porcelain. Her scales shone silvery blue in the sunshine like a thousand nacreous pieces of mirror. But where her legs should have been, she was slippery and squamous as a fish.

Wondering how to win her, Faeroes closed his eyes shyly – and sang loudly and with all his heart:

'Sweet princess, I've loved you dearly
For half an hour, or very nearly.'

Then, overcome, he couldn't continue.

But it worked; the Mermaiden laughed, and was his.

Faeroes carried her back to his Castle in the air and made her his Queen - though aware that Fair Isle was a fickle Mermaiden, full of sea-secrets that even he didn't know.

And Weather-making was, for the Mermaiden, a simple pleasure. If she had an idea for a hot day, she'd grow misty, fall into a reverie, then give such a clear tinkling laugh, that sailors hearing it across the seas would be entranced. And even if she just thought about the sea, a warm Summer shower would appear.

Faeroes knew the water element ran strongly in her, like changing currents. Sometimes, when you were talking to her, she might give a flip of her tail and leave. This was not rudeness – just the way Mermaids behave. But Faeroes feared that one day she might flip into the sea from the Castle walls, dive down into the Deep ... and never be seen again. 'And I cannot do without you ...' he thought.

Now his children were growing up. Their girl and boy twins: Thames and Tyne, were alike as two clams ... except for one thing: Thames, the girl, had a small flapping Mermaiden's tail.

Faeroes heaved with emotion as he watched.

'Surely, everything's all right? Surely?' ... But it was not.

A piercing shriek from the Hall came from Nanny Dover, who appeared on the balcony in a shower of talcum powder, which immediately condensed around her.

'Have you heard the dreadful news? I've just read it in yesterday's copy of 'The Sun'. A mysterious Weather-crime has been committed: a Weather-kidnap; oh it's Awful!'

'Calm down Nanny! Calm down!' Faeroes shushed.

Barely a moment later, Fastnet whizzed up from below, her face crinkled with concern.

NANNY DOVER
In charge of the Castle children

'The BBC have just made an announcement; they're searching for a young girl, Wendy, snatched from the roof of the Met Office ... by the Weather!'

'What do you mean 'by the weather?'

Faeroes looked from one to the other, his heart beating far too fast.

'A small Tornado, apparently ... she was snatched inside a Tornado and...'

'Yes, it's all here, in 'The Sun', plain as daylight,' Nanny butted in. 'Do let me read it out – and do stop telling me to calm down:

"A young school-girl was today whipped off the roof of the Exeter Meteorological Station during an Exhibition being staged there. The missing girl's friend, Raine, stated:

"I saw a long spiralling tube of dark grey come right out of the blue, wrap itself around Wendy, and just carry her off in a North-Westerly direction."

The young girl's mother is frantic, as you can imagine,' Nanny added. 'Wait, there's more...

"When Wendy's Mother was shown some pages from 'The Observer's Book of Weather', Raine pointed straight at a picture of a Tornado. "Yes, that's what it was," she stated.'

'Look at the date, Nanny. That happened two days ago,' said Plymouth, joining them from her sun-bed. Papers like 'The Sun' always take ages to get here by air-mail, what with the post as it is nowadays.'

'We'll talk about it more over High Tea,' Faeroes announced. 'It smells as if the sardines-on-toast are more than ready. Oh dear! Presumably, Finisterre's had one of her Depressions again; she normally produces more inventive food. Sound the Dinner-Gong would you, Fastnet.'

PLYMOUTH
Hot sunshine and
Anticyclones

In the Dining-room, Wizard Wight was busily discussing the kidnapping affair with Fisher; Fair Isle was complaining to Nanny that she'd dropped a great number of stitches from hearing the news.

Plymouth and Forties were attempting to settle the twins on their chairs. They'd grown fractious with the disturbed atmosphere.

Finally, when Dogger and Bailey, the two Weather Sentinels, came in, they had to be told the news all over again. And Finisterre arrived with yet more burnt sardines on toast for them. No wonder the assembled company looked overcast. She was meant to be producing Cordon Bleu Cookery …

Faeroes, standing patiently at the head of the table, signalled to Plymouth to say Grace. Perhaps that might settle them:

Plymouth nodded and rose to her feet. Sweeping back her long fair hair she sang it sweetly in B flat minor, staring rather angrily towards their wayward

Cordon Bleu Cook:

'Thank you for the clear blue sky,
May our pressures all be High.
Help us battle with our foes
To dispel all dreadful Lows.
Please stop Finisterre from sending
Foul Depressions never-ending.
May our outlooks all be bright,
Oil pollution bravely fight.
Let us all make perfect weather:
Sunny spells that last forever.
Try to let us not complain ...
*Burnt sardines on toast **again**.'*

'This is most alarming,' Wizard Wight said. 'The direction this Tornado took was towards Heligoland wasn't it?'

'Yes, it has to be Heligoland's doing,' said Dogger. 'What in Heavens are they are up to! It's absolutely against all Sky Laws and Celestial Regulations to capture an Earthling. It's a most unnatural state of affairs.'

'Well, if an Earthling is at Heligoland Hall, then she'll have to be rescued – and at once,' Faeroes insisted. 'This is appalling news. Dogger and Bailey, you two Weather Sentinels must be sent out while our calm weather holds. See if you can spy what's going on. And search for our lost Kittiwake on the way, too if you can. Forties will form a small cloud – a Cumulus Humilis – for you both to travel on inconspicuously.'

'As for you, Finisterre - I'm afraid we're no longer able to put up with your Depressions. You've dampened our power considerably. We've been unable to make any Fair Weather strong enough to combat a whole year's Foul Weather from Heligoland. Such behaviour cannot be tolerated at Beaufort any longer.

I hereby banish you from the Castle.'

While their Cordon Bleu Cook angrily packed her things, King Faeroes announced: 'No-one is to mention Finisterre again – or visit her – wherever she decides to reside. Is that clear?'

'Clear as daylight,' they all chanted.

Filling her cloud-duvet-cover with personal belongings, and swinging this over her shoulder, Finisterre stormed from the castle on her own Backing Wind.

But, before leaving, she pulled out her wand and pointing it at her own uneaten burnt sardines, declared angrily. 'Well, if I have to go – from now on, you, Fisher, will only be able to catch sardines – and it'll be sardines on toast for you all at EVERY MEAL!'

With a heavy heart, and in a tearful state, Finisterre blew straight down to Earth, to the only person she knew would be able to help her.

Chapter 7
Portland Bill

Portland Bill was forever polishing and cleaning parts of his Lighthouse: there was always an oily rag in his hands. The Beam from his Lighthouse was said to be the brightest in the land. For it guided passing vessels through the hazardous waters off the Island of Portland, as well as acting as a way-mark for ships navigating the English Channel.

Finisterre tethered her Mare to a sturdy rock and, carrying her possessions for safety, puffed up the 153 steps that lead to the top of Portland Bill's Lighthouse. Each step grew heavier and heavier as she wound round and round, higher and higher, to reach his Lamp Room. She was not used to walking on Earth: its gravity was tiresome.

Portland Bill knew of the existence of the Fair Weather-Makers, from information gathered by all the Sea-Birds over his years as Lighthouse Keeper. And so, when Finisterre burst through into his Lamp Room and sank exhausted onto the floor asking for his help, he almost looked as if he was expecting her.

'I'll help you, Finisterre, if I can,' he reassured her... quickly ... noting that the atmosphere around her was becoming grey with her Depressive state, threatening to fog out the flashes from his Lighthouse Lamp. So he comfort-ed her with a cup of his strong hot tea and waited until the grey mist cleared, so that she was able to tell of her banishment.

'I do know a little about your problem already. You suffer from a Split Personality, don't you - if I'm right?'

'Yes, Portland, you're such a wise Therapist. You see it's like this: ever since I was a child, I imagined for myself a companion - a masculine part of myself – which I called 'Fitzroy'. But as I grew, so did Fitzroy – and he opposes me now at every turn. I feel he's taking me over more and more.'

'Finisterre, I know all about your history, and I have to reveal to you – as those who knew about it seem to have carefully covered the sorry story up, or more likely you were too young to understand – that your dear Mother, Gaia Celeste, was abducted by the Foul Wizard Cromarty from Heligoland. For this behaviour, he was blown entirely away - but your Mother died giving birth to twins: one she called Finisterre, the other, Hebrides. You were the Fair one – but have Foul tendencies; Hebrides is Foul but may have some Fair tendencies.'

'Oh!' exclaimed Finisterre; then added in a lower, frightened voice, 'So that's why I'm the way I am: half Foul, half Fair. And presumably it's this Foul part of myself I call Fitzroy who's the cause of all the Depressions I keep having.'

'That is so,' Portland Bill nodded.

'So it must have been Fitzroy, too, who caused me to evaporate Captain Humber's wife, Shannon, when we clashed head on with her in Mid Atlantic last year, and refused to let me blow by.
And that's the reason we've been punished at Beaufort with all this year's continual Foul Weather.'

'Indeed, yes. That is so. Perhaps I can give you a little Light Therapy. That might help you?' he suggested, kindly.

Portland laid Finisterre's head next to his lighthouse's massive lamp - on the landward side so its message wouldn't be obscured for ships at sea - and gave her bursts of 20 second flashes in groups of 4.

The intensity of 635,000 candelas had an astounding effect. Finisterre collapsed senseless onto the floor.

Portland Bill hoped his Light Therapy had not been too much for Finisterre's sensitive disposition. And although very preoccupied with flashing his lamp to prevent shipping from being thrown onto the rocks during the terrible storm raging from the Irish Sea, he kept a Weather-eye on her throughout the night while he went about his work.

When Finisterre awoke, feeling bright and glowing with health, she'd heard nothing of the storm. And when presented with another cup of strong tea, she saw that her tarnished wand – which she'd only used for raising a subsiding soufflé or two – had been polished to a radiant silver.
Then her eyes lighted on the orb left to her by her Mother. This, too, had been polished up clear as crystal. She'd only used this at Beaufort Castle to prevent her Cordon Bleu recipes from being blown away. She was delighted.

'Finisterre, listen. You have within you the powers of a White Witch … and they're unimaginable powers inherited from your Mother. Go away and use them. Use your wand to build yourself a new residence. Use your orb to see what's afoot. Believe in your new powers – you may find some not yet used. Use your knowledge of lotions and potions for the good of others – you have inherited powers of healing from Gaia Celeste, which you've never discovered in yourself.'

Full of gratitude, Finisterre tried out her newly-polished wand for the first time, by touching his line of empty Brasso and Silvo tins, filling them anew to the brim.

'Thank you, dear Finisterre … and there is something else I need you to do, now that you've had this Light Therapy. While you were restoring yourself overnight, my Birds informed me of some terrible news: an Earthling Girl has been captured and carried away to Heligoland for their own use. She has with her an extremely dangerous book by one Johann Heinrich Lambert. It is evil! It contains Cabalistic symbols, which can be used to produce harmful weather-patterns for our whole planet. If you ever come across it, you must Destroy it straight away. For it shows the reader how to manufacture **'Extreme Weather Conditions.'**

'And if you can rescue this Earthling Girl, too, she must be returned safely to Earth - onto the roof of the Meteorological Station in Exeter – as soon as possible'.

'Thank you, I'll try my very best.'

As Finisterre gathered her things together and made her farewell, Portland gave her one final piece of advice:

'Remember, Finisterre, you must always keep yourself positive and strong. For if you weaken in a negative way, Fitzroy may be able to take over your personality once again.'

Feeling full of her new power, Finisterre mounted her Backing Wind, and blew South-West towards her own Sea-Area off Cap Finisterre – a place where she felt comfortable and at home with herself.

There, choosing a sky-space, she swirled her shiny wand in the air, and wished for a gloriously-fashionable Cirrostratus Residence to appear exactly in this Very Enviable Location, North of the Azores.

At once her spell was granted.

Silver spangles of light showered from her wand, bathing the sky around in sparkling enchantment. And there right in front of her, materialized an architectural masterpiece in High Rococo –

'I name you Sunny Intervals', Finisterre declared.

After that, the new White Witch went happily around, spending almost all of the wand's energy furnishing the new residence in her own artistic style, including a wardrobe of her own personal fashions and a clinic for her Natural Remedies.

But, thinking she might have used too much power on material, rather than spiritual things, Finisterre put the wand to recharge, using electro-magnetic waves.

Chapter 8
Dogger and Bailey

E arly the next morning, the two Weather Sentinels, Dogger and Bailey, set off from Beaufort Castle on a small Cumulus Humilis Fair Weather cloud which Forties the Cloud-Maker had manufactured for them. They hid them selves on its fluff, and had it pushed along by a gentle South-Easterly breeze.

Visibility was excellent, the sky unusually calm, the deep blue of the water's stillness below mirrored by brighterer blue sky above. Peering over the edge of their Cumulus, they could see the outline of England looking very flat and rather like a Weather-map.

Later, when their Cumulus reached the Bristol Channel, they they turned North-West over Mumbles Lighthouse to begin their Spying Mission.

DOGGER and BAILEY
Weather Sentinels

But the nearer they approached Heligoland Hall, in the middle of the Irish Sea, the more nervous they became.

So they took a long draft of sardine soup from their vacuum flask … and both sighed, remembering how, when she was a Cordon Bleu cook for Beaufort, Finisterre's warm spells used to be enchanting, her heat-waves always working like charms – and she had a magical way with Thermals.

49

Everything she cooked had been executed with such fine flourish. And with her masterful manipulation of air, her gateaux never flopped, her soufflés always rose beautifully.

'I'm already really bored with Sardines,' moaned Bailey.

So Dogger decided on some of his Doggerel to keep his friend from fretting as they sailed along, and it managed - in its quirky way - to make him laugh:

And now to you we will relate
Just how the Fish got to the plate
And was devoured at such a rate
By the man who couldn't wait
Until he'd eaten all the Skate.
And about the woman who
Put together two and two
Rushed downstairs at such a rate
So she wouldn't be too late
Saw a very empty dish
Standing there without its fish
Other things she quickly noted
Saw a man completely bloated
Snoring in an easy chair
Grabbed him roughly by the hair
Flew into a fearful rage
Beat him soundly for an age
And with that not quite contented
Growing all the while demented
Grasped the dish with both her hands
On his head the whole thing lands
Brings the man back to his senses
And with her he fights and fences
But she gets the upper hand
Gives the man to understand
He must fully compensate
For the lovely piece of Skate
Ninety pennies he must pay
Then she lets him run away

And she can't control her laughter
For she's heard of nothing dafter
Knew the fish was slightly high
Now she's got enough to buy
Two fresh fish instead of one
And a dish to put them on

But his laughter was interrupted by a shrill call…

'Scree! Scree!' coming from immediately below.

Bailey quickly leaned over the cloud-edge to see what the fuss was about, rocking it dangerously.

'Careful! You'll have us over!' said Dogger. 'Let me look.'

Carefully, pressing the cloud-fluff aside, he saw a large Guillemot in a terrible flap right below them.

Moments later, the Sea-Bird landed on the edge of the Cumulus, then took off again and circled their heads lamenting.

'My friend is dying. Help me! Scree! Scree!'

'Hush now, Guillemot, Hush!' Dogger ordered the agitated bird. 'Tell your tale more slowly, then maybe we can help.'

The Sea-Bird landed, ruffled its feathers and, in staccato phrases, explained:

'I fly along. Spot this poor floating Sea-Bird drifting from enemy waters off Heligoland. Dive low. Hardly recognize my friend, Kittiwake, in such a black sticky mess. I think dead. Poke her with my beak. She opens eyes.

"Quick, WAR!" she cries. "Beaufort's in danger! Windy, is captured! Rescue her… or my Earthling friend will die in the dungeon. Warn Beaufort … or we'll all be killed!" Then she flops her head again.'

The Guillemot would not be still and continued in a terrible flap: 'you have to help or they'll die! Scree! Scree!'

So the two Weather Sentinels tried to persuade the Cumulus Humilis to fall to just above sea level.

The cloud was reluctant; it thought a sudden drop in altitude might cause too much evaporation and diminish its size.

But after Dogger promised to upgrade its rank from Cumulus to Altocumulus as a reward, the small cloud eventually agreed. It tried really hard and was able to reach sea level without losing too much substance.

With the aid of Baily's wide belt, they hoisted Kittiwake aboard.

51

Kittiwake appeared to be dead, but when Bailey put one of his shiny tunic buttons to her beak, it clouded over.

'We must return to Beaufort before it's too late,' he pronounced gravely.

'No!' The Sea-Bird insisted, 'Only Finisterre can save Kittiwake. Squark!'

'But we're not supposed to visit her now she's been banished. We don't even know where she's gone.'

'Follow me, then, Squark! Finisterre's powerful now - a White Witch! Her Residence is new, too. Squark!
We must travel South-West, to her own Sea Area. Squark! Squark!'

'But the wind's blowing entirely in the wrong direction to travel South,' Bailey pointed out.

'Nevertheless, it's got to be done,' Dogger insisted. And when Dogger made up his mind, being a dogged character, there was nothing much you could do about it.

So, breaking all the rules of Cloud Conduct and Good Etiquette of the Skies, the little Cumulus Humilis raced off as fast as it was able across the blue, with Guillemot flying ahead.

It did look funny travelling the opposite direction to all the other small Cumulus clouds, and it had to move down into a different wind-stratum to avoid being smashed to smithereens.

Normally, clouds don't have to work hard to go along: the wind does it for them. They merely carry water. But, what with the weight of the two Weather Sentinels, plus the injured Sea-Bird, it had to push so hard against the prevailing wind that, by the time they neared Cap Finisterre, the curly bits had been squashed out behind in a long tail, and the front rounded off a bit … so it looked more like a meteor flying along.

Chapter 9
White Witch Extraordinary.

F inisterre, glanced through her lancet window later that evening and spied her first visitors. They arrived, she thought, on rather a tatty Cumulus, which landed rather clumsily on her new cloud-Lawn. But she was delighted to see that they were the Weather Sentinels from Beaufort.

Down her cloud-cut steps she flew on the tips of her new high-heeled crystal shoes, greeting them with outstretched arms, her fishnet gown fashioned with abalone fragments floating out behind. The final rays of sunset, finding the corners of her new rhinestone spectacles, sparkled there in little sunsets of their own; her beautiful face filled with pleasure as she reached them.

'Darlings, do come in. How lovely to see you. Hasn't it been gorgeous today after Heligoland's awful storm last night?'

'Oh!' she exclaimed, as she saw the bedraggled bird. 'The poor thing! Come in side at once; all of you!'

Bailey held Kittiwake in his arms, and Guillemot rest ed on Dogger's shouder as they climbed the new stratified steps to her front door. Pools of silver from an ascend ing moon sunk porously into the cloud-lawn. It burnished the trembling water-droplets condensing on the spires.

FINISTERRE- the-WHITE WITCH/FITZROY
Cordon Bleu Cook for Beaufort Castle and Fitzroy, her male 'other half'

Dogger and Bailey were astounded at the change

in Finisterre. She was so strong and entrancing, and her new Residence: absolutely enchanting! Walking through the entrance was like a visit to Paradise. Heavenly music, designed to lower stress, filtered through every room, seeping from sponge-speakers lodged high in the ceiling.

Finisterre told them she was now a White Witch: very powerful - and with a newly-charged wand and orb.

'Also, I've inherited all my Mother's powers, and can use my new 'Clinic of Natural Remedies' to cure the Sea-Birds.

So I'll be able to restore Kittiwake, I hope. Come this way.'

Finisterre searched through her Herbals, concentrating in a positive way as Portland Bill had instructed:

… Iodine, Potassium, Iron, Vitamin B12, Calcium …

She ground these together with powdered kelp in her pestle and mortar.

Finally, the mixture was moistened with a little sea-cucumber juice to make a 'Rescue Remedy'.

But first she uncorked a vial of 'Squid's ink with Ozone' and, holding this beneath Kittiwake's beak, watched for a reaction.

With a huge frightened SQUARK! the Sea-Bird revived.

And when she saw where she was, and that Guillemot was still with her, Kittiwake gabbled, 'I was inside the Barnacle Jelly. I overheard everything. German Bight's captured a poor Earthling girl called Windy … She's the Guardian of a Tome to form Weather Spells. It's for War against Beaufort.'

Finisterre trembled at the news … though she didn't quite understand the jelly part … but the Tome part she had been warned about from Portland.

'You did well, Kittiwake, but now you must rest. We'll take action to warn Beaufort Castle as soon as we can. You're lucky, this tarry soot saved you from sinking.'

She talked soothingly to the Sea-Bird while skilfully applying splints of Gull's feathers to the broken leg and wing.

After that, Finisterre stroked Kittiwake's head gently, until she sank into a painless trance. Only then did the White Witch's gentle eyes moisten with tears. 'There's nothing you three can do 'til tomorrow either. Now we'll eat and rest.'

Finisterre treated them to Celestial Soup, Frumenty and Angel Cake; and, although her guests felt sad and grave, this meal reminded them of the old

Cordon Bleu cooking days before the White Witch started having her Depressions. Finisterre showed them to their new rooms – the Pearl and the Coral. (Guillemot preferred to roost on the heated bathroom rail.)

Soon they were fast asleep ... but the new White Witch's work had barely begun.

While her visitors slept, Finisterre climbed the spiral stairs to her central Onion Dome. She was filled with despair about this unlawful act from Heligoland, and the time had come to consult her new crystal orb - to see beyond herself. She needed to confirm Kittiwake's news.

Opening the curved door to a circular room, painted in delicate shades of pink and furnished in mother-of-pearl, she reached the orb on a central table. Composing herself, she sat still in front of it until she felt neutral.

Her new crystal would make a celestial eye into which she could peer into the heart of things.

Drawing out a powder-blue silk cloth from the table drawer, she slowly polished the surface, uttering a soft incantation to erase time and reality.

Reading the crystal would take a lot of energy; but, as she rubbed the orb, it grew warm, taking on a faint glow, an inner luminescence. Harder she pressed, while her chant gained volume and speed.

The glow increased to an incandescence.

Soon the whole room radiated with ultra-violet, filtering in a blue smoky light through the misty windows and out into the night.

As the energy intensified, the mother-of-pearl furniture sent prisms of light streaking off Finisterre's dress, to bounce against the strawberry walls in smouldering showers. Never had Finisterre felt so powerful, never so excited. Mauve sparks flew from the turret and shot towards the stars. 'Ouch!' she cried angrily, as positive currents made her fizz. Her orb had clouded over.

Finisterre bent forward in concentration.

All at once the crystal cleared. A thin Earthling with wild, unruly hair was curled up, hugging her knees tightly, and shut inside what looked like a damp dungeon at sea level.

'Oh, the poor thing! And she's only dressed in a shirt and jeans. Had she already been frozen to death by that terrible storm? No, I see she moves a little in her sleep. But she has to be rescued fast ... or the Foul atmosphere will surely kill her.'

Again the crystal clouded over, then cleared to show a Black Witch and a monocled gentleman pouring over what had to be Johann Heinrich Lambert's Tome, pointing out various strange symbols, working out some kind of Equation.

Finisterre frowned. This was the very Tome that Portland Bill urged her to destroy as soon as she could. But how?

'If the Foul Weather-Makers have this evil book,' she thought, 'there's no knowing what destructive forces could be manufactured from it ... probably bad enough to destroy Beaufort Castle, the Fair Weather-Makers, the Earthlings ... even the planet itself. Indeed, it could bring upon us all the most destructive Weather War.'

Finisterre was filled with horror. What would occur if the planet itself were altered? She found herself growing far too disturbed ... could no longer watch what the orb was telling her. Her concentration faltered; the orb faded out.

She wiped her hot brow with the silken cloth, then put it away. Portland Bill had warned her of this treachery... but how difficult it was to remain positive after what she had just viewed.

As she descended the stairs, Finisterre was smitten with a great pity for that poor Earthling. She'd always wanted a daughter of her own. And although she had always loved and wanted a child with dear Fisher at Beaufort, who loved her, she realized that he would never be capable of taking on both her – and Fitzroy.

Also, she was perturbed at the idea of having to help the Fair Weather-Makers - when they'd only just banished her ...

'Maybe I could just delay Heligoland's preparations somehow, so that Beaufort has time to construct some War Weather of its own. Oh dear! I'm beginning to feel so odd, so changeable ... and I can't fight it ... can't fight it ...'

It didn't help matters that the moon was almost full that night - a most troublesome time for Finisterre emotionally - as she tended to wax and wane with that Lunar Body.

Long before midnight, she suffered a full Temperature Inversion and knew that one of her 'turns' was imminent. She must stay calm; must remain positive - as Portland Bill had said she should.

Quickly, she climbed into the comfort of her luxury oyster-bed … before another Depression could develop.

But before Finisterre was even aware of it … the Fitzroy part of herself had taken advantage of her lowered, exhausted state.

He was not going to be supressed so easily – and she'd let her guard down already!

Soon he was in command.

Soon he was up and dressed in jodhpurs.

Soon he was down in the new stables, harnessing Finisterre's Backing Wind.

Grabbing her new wand, he tore through the skies, and found he was veering towards Heligoland, drawn along by powerful negative forces.

And the going was so easy: bright stars shone in the clear vault of the heavens; a moon, practically full, formed a silver runway for him across the ocean.

A while later, he noticed that the horizon off Cap Finisterre had darkened into a huge area of BLACK. Why? What was it?

Then, as he approached nearer still, he saw right below the Backing Wind, an enormous oil tanker.

It had been scored badly along its side by some jagged rock – 'probably wrecked by that Black Witch Hebrides during their colossal storm last night,' he thought.

Seeping from the tanker was an ooze of thick, black, treacly oil, lying suspended on an unusually calm Irish Sea.

Flying lower still, Fitzroy contemplated this event for a while, then he had the most treacherous idea.

Taking Finisterre's newly-polished wand, he encouraged her Backing Wind to descend right down to sea level, pointing towards the blackness. Next, he conjured up a Foul spell: one that would counteract his other half's new positive thinking.

'Pollution is the Solution,' he pronounced.

There was not much energy left in the wand - but just enough to set the huge slick heading very slowly and steadily, so it wouldn't break up, towards the direction of Heligoland Hall.

Off it went, creeping like a great carpet of evil over the surface of the sea.

Fitzroy returned his Wind-Force to the new Stables back at Sunny Intervals, changed quickly back into her negligée, and fell exhausted onto their oyster bed.

When Finisterre awoke the following day, she felt unnaturally weary and drained of energy. She'd dreamed of riding … riding along to a terrible dark place.

But, pulling herself together, she knew exactly what she had to do: she wrote an important message and - for safety's sake – copied it, tying each part securely to the feet of her two best Rock Pigeons. These she sent off to Beaufort Castle from her Northern Turret.

After that, she went to her stables and trimmed and reined two Force 5 Winds, ready for her guests. She noticed her own Backing Wind looking very out of sorts, snorting, short of puff, and seriously diminished. Sadly, she wondered whether her favourite Wind-Force had got too old to blow for very much longer. She let her out to chew for a while on some of her new white cloud-lawn.

Once the White Witch had finished all preparations, she woke the Weather-Sentinels and gave them a breakfast of Starfish-on-Toast.

Kittiwake had come round from her trance and could work her wing – but not enough to fly. Her leg was still very weak, but mending – though she could neither walk nor perch.

'Listen carefully everyone,' Finisterre said. 'Although my wand tiresomely seems to need re-charging yet again, there's enough energy left for what I require. I've touched the Cumulus Humilis you came on, elevating it to an Altostratus. Guillemot, I want you to hide Kittiwake in its fluff, and sail her down to the Bird Sanctuary at Maplin Sands on Earth, where she can convalesce. After that, it's imperative that you warn all Fair Sea-Birds to fly only in close-convoy flocks from now on - for their own safety.'

'You, Dogger and Bailey, can return to Beaufort on these two Force 5 Winds. What Kittiwake says is all perfectly true. I've already sent out warnings - but give Beaufort an additional message from me: tell the Fair Weather-Makers to make preparations for War as fast as they are able.

As for me, I have to go to Heligoland.'

'Heligoland!' They stared at her in disbelief. But Finisterre's eyes had grown strangely hard and her shoulders looked very broad; so they knew there was nothing more to be said.

Quickly they thanked her and made their farewells.

As Dogger and Bailey sped onwards to Beaufort, so keen were they to hurry back that they failed to notice a flock of black shapes approach and, like flickering shadows, follow them home.

But two evil Shags had been watching with interest the ultra-violet escaping from the White Witch's Onion Dome in the night, and decided to wing around and investigate further. They later witnessed an extremely Foul-looking Finisterre blow furiously on her Backing Wind from the Residence, far faster than they could follow, later still returning on that same Backing Wind.

Finally, just as a glazed sun was ascending in the East, they saw Finisterre send out two Rock Pigeons from her Northern Turret.

The Shags promptly set off after the Fair-Weather Pigeons, attacking them from above. One Pigeon was able to escape - though they'd managed to tear off half the message from its leg. Then it flew as fast as it could, heading South-East towards the safety of Beaufort Castle.

But the Shags, working as a team, managed to overcome the other Pigeon, then set off at top speed in the opposite direction towards Heligoland Hall, the poor Pigeon trapped between them.

Over the bright blue sea, a small scared Rock Pigeon faltered in her flight, trying to hide the remains of the message the White Witch had tied to one foot. Her dark round eyes were wide and watchful as she travelled alone in fear of her feathers, avoiding any flock of Sea-Birds she saw.

But her energy was slipping away from her as she made for the Beaufort Dovecote, wondering what had happened to her friend.

Chapter 10
The Torn Message

Beaufort was enjoying a third day when they'd been able to make Fair Weather easily. Forties was working away, manufacturing a fresh lot of Fair-Weather clouds, while Finisterre's Rock Pigeons fluttered and cooed around his head.

FORTIES
Cloud maker, clouds and Rock Pigeons

Ever since Finisterre had been banished, Forties had taken over the responsibility of looking after these gentle Birds. He fed thems mall pieces of Ambrosia and Manna, which kept them healthy, and their feathers white.

But when an exhausted new arrival perched hesitantly at the window, looking nervously around, Forties stopped turning his cloud-making ratchet and shambled over to the window where the small Pigeon stood swaying uncertainly, her feathers all fluffed and flustered, fearfully looking around at the others. She carried rather a ragged message around one foot.

'Hallo, what's this? That's one of her special Pigeons not seen since the banishment, if I'm not mistook. What's she doing flying back to her old Dovecote in such a state?'

Forties carefully scooped the frightened bird in paddle-shaped hands and felt her small heart beating at an astounding rate. He stroked and talked soothingly while he undid what remained of a rather tattered message.

'There now,' he cooed, 'don't you go a-frettin. Quieten while I untie you. Well! Blow me! What's this? A message from Finisterre in her hand-writing! I'd best take it to Wizard White, he'll know how to deal with it better than myself.'

WIZARD WIGHT: Hot Spells and Light Effects

Forties was in great awe of the ancient Wizard, whose over bearing importance was enhanced by a richly-coloured gown, which gave the impression of disturbing an unnecessary amount of air.

'Who's there? I'm not to be interrupted. I'm busy reading:

" ...on moonlit nights, clouds are visible when the moon is only a quarter full... "'

As he read, the Wizard's two emerald eyes pierced the words intently, and his sand-coloured hair brushed across the page. 'What do you want?'

Forties stayed at his Turret door, and delivered his message from there.

But soon, a troubled Wizard was frowning as he read Finisterre's message:

' ... and so I'm going to Heligoland. Keep a look out for Foul Weather-Birds sent as spies. You're all in great danger. The Tome has to be rescued - as well as the Earthling - and find out about Cabalistic signs. F.'

'This doesn't make any sense; the first part seems to be missing. I'd better check things just to make sure.'

Wizard Wight's dark purple gown swirled as he opened his Turret window, allowing a warm breeze to blow into the room, moving some huge mobiles of planets and astral bodies into orbit. He scanned the skies with his telescope.

'No. Nothing ... only Plymouth sunbathing on her cloud-bed, with her long blond hair spread out in strands. The last two days she's enjoyed bleaching it in the Sun's rays. She might well be vain,' he thought, 'but Plymouth has eyes like a Sea-Hawk; she'd have spotted trouble – if there was any.'

He was about to draw his telescope in, when he became aware of shadows, evenly spaced, flickering across Plymouth's sunburnt form. Without hesitation, he swung it up again, just in time to catch a glimpse of a formation of Stormy Petrels, flying very fast in close convoy, high above Beaufort.

'Stars and spangles! I must see Faeroes straight away.'

Plymouth felt the shadows pass over her lids. Usually, she was able to dispel any grey cloud that got between her and the Sun. Now instinct told her this was different. She sat up, shivering and afraid. Grabbing her suntan lotion she, too, went in search of Faeroes.

By the time Fisher had brought up his sardines and sounded the gong for Lunch, the whole assembled company became overcast - and the two Weather Sentinels still hadn't returned. They were never late for Lunch and the Weather wasn't even Foul.

Then, right in the middle of the meal, there was loud blowing, followed by an urgent Weather Report from the Castle Cloud Hailer:

"Two Force Fives, veering sharply from a South-Westerly direction" ...

This announced the arrival of Dogger and Bailey on the ramparts.

With the Weather Sentinels' news, the meal was forgotten.

'The Foul Weather-Makers mean to wage a Weather War using a powerful Equation from Wizard Cromarty's newly-discovered Tome,' announced Bailey, slumping down out of breath.

'They're training their Sea-Birds to form *The Foul Feathered Force*. If we hadn't found a flock of Fair Weather Birds making for the safety of Beaufort, we'd have been shredded to bits,' added a despondent Dogger ... 'and by the way, Finisterre's seems to have deserted us. She's become a powerful White Witch now and told us, in a strange, rather determined voice, that she's off to Heligoland!'

'Nonsense,' Fisher retorted. 'My Finisterre would never do that.'

'It's true,' Wizard Wight confirmed. 'It implies the same on that bit of message delivered by one of her own Pigeons this morning to our Dovecote. You just don't want to believe it.'

'It's probably because we banished her' said Bailey.

'Then it has to be true,' Faeroes sighed, his face clouding over. 'Not only do we have to rescue that poor Earthling – but we, ourselves have to prepare for War.'

'But if there's going to be a Weather War, then Beaufort will get blown apart!' Nanny Dover shrieked. Now no longer able to control her emotions, she burst into tears and led the twins, who were also sobbing, out of the room.

No-one could move. They were shocked into silence. Nanny was bound to be right … she always was.

Chapter 11

Fair Isle

All night long, Fastnet the Castle Secretary, typed out Faeroes' **War Report** on the Cloud Computer.

By 0700 hours Greenwich Mean Time it was finished.

Fastnet usually worked at such High Pressure that nobody could keep up with her. She was responsible for putting clocks forward an hour for Summer, was in charge of all the 'Highs'. She knew the Force of every wind, having learned Admiral Beaufort's Wind-Scale by heart ... she was even quite good at making sardine sandwiches. She never had enough time, and had forgotten to marry.

By 0800 hours, the **War Report** was copied for everyone.

Then Fastnet's elastic figure was seen tearing through the Long Gallery, past Finisterre's picture – which had been turned upside-down in disgrace.

(Fastnet had not been successfully captured for her own picture: there was just one pointed foot, a glimpse of an ill-fitting cardigan, and a lot of vapour).

FASTNET
Castle Secretary;
High Pressure

All Faeroes' Reports were delivered exactly on time for the **War Meeting** to begin.

'This is the greatest blow we could have received,' King Faeroes-the-Good announced. 'I'm afraid we're no longer powerful enough to save Britain from its consequences either. Working against an Equation formed from Wizard Cromarty's Tome will be impossible. The Foul Weather- Makers will be able to construct a lethal climate … and, if they have Finisterre on their side… then her new powers joined to theirs will be greatly magnified.

All we can hope to do is adopt a Defensive Position. We might, indeed, have only enough strength to stop Beaufort blowing apart.'

At that news, a cloud of Anti-cyclonic Gloom spread throughout the room, and the Meeting grew so turbulent that their Leader had to stand on a chair to be seen and heard above the swirling mist.

Faeroes needed to wait until the air cleared enough to continue.

'Yes, creating **War Weather** of our own, is something none of us will relish. So, from now on, the daily workings of the Castle will have to be changed.

Fastnet has typed up for me the following Report:

Fair Isle, you have to create large areas of Calm.

Fastnet, Ridges of very High Pressure.

Plymouth, exceptionally clear blue skies.

Wizard Wight will form strong Sunny Spells.

Forties, you must make massive Cloud Formations.

I, myself, will train the Winds up to higher velocities.

Dogger and Bailey will form our Birds into a Fair Weather Force - an exhausting discipline they'll certainly not enjoy. Fisher, in addition to catching sardines, you'll have to set up a system of Thermographs, Barographs, and Anemographs so we can gauge what's going on.

Lastly, Nanny Dover must start tinning sardines for Wartime Rations - as well as training the children to adopt stringent **Wartime Discipline**.'

And so, Weather-making was accelerated at Beaufort Castle.

That very afternoon, Fisher was seen punching two holes in the cloud, and two fishing-lines fell into the salty water below for extra War-rations.

And here was Nanny Dover coming forward with all the children thoroughly pulled together. She'd started tinning Fisher's extra sardines, too, after sensibly disguising every tear with a liberal dusting of 'English Lavender' spread evenly over face, neck and bosom.

Its chalky appearance prompted Plymouth to refer to those friendly prominences as 'The White Cliffs of Dover', and Nanny, having a great sense of humour, laughed … after which, the Castle atmosphere started to improve.

That night, after their High Tea of sardine soup was sipped, Fair Isle sang to give them all hope. She sang of swallows flying over the sea; of Summer and the sailing-ships at Cowes. She looked very pretty leaning forward at her harp, and before long, visibility was returned almost to normal.

But while Fisher was doing his double fishing, the following day, he turned his mind back to the old days… days when his dignity and pride were unquestioned, his character impeccable, his bravery undaunted, and his powers of endurance remarkable. All this was to impress Finisterre, whom he loved. Yes, it was HE who volunteered for dangerous missions to the Equator, where the length of daylight throughout the year remained mysteriously the same. It was HE who could identify a wadi; HE who endured beri beri, caught malaria, suffered swamp fever – and survived. But since she'd spurned him and put such a spiteful spell on his rod, so he could only catch sardines, his brightness had dimmed, and he knew he'd never more be seen in Equatorial circles. How he longed for those days when he danced round and round with her in the Beaufort

FISHER
Weather equipment,
calm weather
and fishing

Ballroom. How good we were together, he recalled …

But just then, an exceptional idea interrupted his reverie, like a sardine caught by surprise on his line – one so good he'd announce it at High Tea that evening.

Instead of a Grace before that meal, Nanny Dover tried to prepare them all for War by reading Important Information she found from an ancient copy of: *'The Observer's Book of Weather':*

' *"If caught in a thunderstorm, the recommended procedure is to throw away the golf-clubs, fishing-rods, umbrellas etc. then lie flat on the ground in the open, far away from trees and preferably on a rubber raincoat ..."* '

A useless book, they all chided her as they sat down… nothing but a Fairy Story. No sense to them up here in the air.

'Hear me, please,' Fisher interrupted. 'I've thought of a clever strategy.' He rose to his feet and, with eyes brightening his handsome weather-beaten face, turned to deliver a stunning idea.

And everyone took notice of Fisher's proposals, as he was a really wise Weather-Maker who worked on difficult meteorological problems while he fished, using Zen philosophy. Once these were solved, he could work in the ensuing stillness to reach periods of great Calm.

'While fishing today, I tried to focus all my old energies, and came to this conclusion: why don't we just allow the Foul Weather-Makers to produce all the daily weather … and not try to make any ourselves …while we make weather secretly for War?'

'A brilliant idea! Well done!' Wizard Wight's eyes sparkled. 'I could form a cloud of Anti-cyclonic Gloom to go just around Beaufort Castle, behind which we could be constructing our different weather for War.'

'This idea is good, we'll start first thing tomorrow,' Faeroes announced.

So, the following morning, an urgent variety of noises of a kind never heard before filled the atmosphere:

Dogger and Bailey marched Flocks of a Fair Feathered Force in tight formation along the rampart walls.

Fastnet spun herself into a whirlwind to create hot thermals.

The heavy breathing on the cloud-top was Plymouth doing press-ups (instead of her usual Yoga) in preparation for perfect blue skies.

Even Fair Isle managed to increase her warm little showers into greater falls of rain.

Banks of Finisterre's Rock Pigeons rose into the air, frantic with the noise of Forties churning out and stacking up huge, extraordinary clouds: 'Weird'uns - like I've never tried making before,' he muttered, as the ratchets lurched to the unaccustomed strain.

Up in Wizard Wight's Turret, the astral orbs clashed in confusion with other heavenly bodies as the Professor of Fine Celestial Arts flung open chests to search for symbols and spells of the right potency for War.

From the balcony came the quieter concentrated chip-chipping from Nanny Dover and the children as they sat in a circle fashioning Wind Arrows of astonishing sharpness.

And all this was happening behind Wizard Wight's extensive camouflage curtain of Anticyclonic Gloom.

But, as Fisher brought his day's catch in for High Tea, Fair Isle rose up on her mirrored-sparkling tail, and leaning for support on the chair before her, frowned as she admonished them all soundly.

'We've all been thinking about saving ourselves – and Beaufort Castle' (here she glared at Nanny Dover) - 'but what about a Rescue Plan first for that poor Earthling girl? You all seem to have forgotten about her. We cannot leave her to perish in that Foul place a moment longer while we make weather secretly for a War?' (Being a mother, Fair Isle could not imagine leaving the poor mortal to expire). 'What are we going to do? Think, everybody. Think!'

Fisher jumped to his feet. 'Well, I have to tell you all what I intend to do: I've made a decision. Something's just not quite right about my Finisterre, and I mean to fix it. I'm going as a spy to Heligoland Hall first thing tomorrow. I know Finisterre better than any of you. I neither believe that half-note sent to us by a Pigeon, saying that Finisterre had gone to Heligoland. I know she wouldn't desert us.

I'll tell her we've forgiven her, and then get both her and the Earthling back here. I admit I've grown weaker and lost a lot of my brightness since her departure, but allow me to try this, please.'

'Then you may borrow my cloak for protection,' offered Wizard Wight, generously.

'Wait!' Faeroes commanded, 'I've decided to go there myself as a spy. I should've done so a lot earlier – I am your King.'

'No!' cried Fair Isle from the balcony. 'You're not to leave Beaufort!' Her face had drained pale as the moon. 'As King, you're needed here to lead us into battle. Besides, with the skies so full of the Foul Weather Force trained to peck us to death, it's far too dangerous for anybody to go above the waves. That is why I've decided that it's me who has to go there.'

And before anyone could stop her, Fair Isle scattered the whole of Fisher's slippery sardine catch behind her to prevent them following. Then she flipped on to the battlements and dived over the cloud edge and was gone.

Faeroes froze with shock, then collapsed onto the cloud-floor. The one thing he'd most feared had happened. He knew he'd never see his lovely wife again.

At once the Barometer in the Hall jammed; the air grew thick and static. Dogger ran about issuing a Fog Warning. Soon it was as if the whole place had fallen into some kind of vacuum -

A vacuum in which Beaufort's inhabitants could no longer do any work.

Part Three
Pink Champagne

Chapter 12

Malin the Spy

Wendy had not expired in the Dungeon at Heligoland Hall: the warmer weather prevented her from freezing to death.

But tears kept welling up, which she brushed angrily away.

'There has to be some way to get out of this terrible Dungeon. How dare they treat me like this just because I didn't understand Grandpa's book!'

All day after the great storm had spent itself she sat, racking her brains while chewing on the ropey piece of seaweed that served as her belt to stop the pangs of hunger. But she only became thinner and thinner, and no way out of her situation came to mind.

Every so often she went to look through the window-bars of her grille, searching the filmy bands of vapour outside. But a swirling fog-cloud had formed around Heligoland Hall, which she presumed was put there to block her view.

Later on, though, she heard loud commands from the lady with the Weather-map headscarf as she gave shrill orders to flocks of Foul Weather-Birds sweeping overhead in tight ranks. And there came louder noises like the ringing of a hammer on an anvil.

Then, at last, came different calls: harsh screeches and a terrified lamenting, as two large black Sea-Birds flew through the foggy barrier, with a smaller struggling bird captured between them.

The poor thing looked very like an ordinary Pigeon, and had a bit of paper tied around one leg.

'Let that poor bird go!' Wendy bravely shouted through the bars.

But they'd already disappeared from view.

The two Shags pecked at the Kitchen window to let their prisoner in, eager to receive a reward from Lundy after such a tiresome journey from Cap Finisterre.

Seeing the plump Fair Weather-Bird brought to her - she presumed as a 'gift' - Lundy flung open the window, grabbed the Pigeon by its feet, swung it upside down, and plunged it straight into the pot. 'Good, this'll give added flavouring to my Atlantic Soup.'

The Soup seethed and tumbled, swallowing the extra flavour without a murmur. In seconds, the message tied around the Pigeon's foot dissolved and made its way to the surface, where it was skimmed off by Lundy's ladle and thrown away.

Terrified of suffering the same fate, the two Shags made off fast, angry that Lundy seemed to reward them when she felt like it.

Then, spotting Biscay beneath, resting from forming her Feathered Force, they flew down to deliver their news to her instead.

Perhaps she'd reward them ...?

'Finisterre's a White Witch now! We went spying on her. She's really powerful now!' crarked one.

'She's banished from Beaufort but got a great Castle of her own, high in the Cirrostratus. It's called Sunny Intervals,' crarked the other...

'Strange bright sparkles went spinning off from her Turret window. X-rays, Ultra-violet too. Whole area's filled with magic!' crarked the first.

'Later, she raced out, coming towards here on her Backing-Wind – too fast to follow ... then decided to return again!' crarked the second.

'What's more ... she knows about our War!'

Biscay frowned at their news. 'Well done, Shags. Fly round to Lundy to collect some titbits for your brilliant spying news.'

The two Shags didn't feel like being turned upside down and put in Lundy's pot as well. They felt really robbed of their reward, and flew off through the fog screeching and complaining loudly.

Biscay ran quickly inside, calling for the others.

'Rumours have been circulating over the Air-stream,' she announced. 'Listen to this!' She then proceeded to tell them the Shags' extraordinary news.

'How ever did she get wind of our War? Somehow, she must've become far more powerful than we ever imagined,' said Humber.

'Was Finisterre really racing to join us later on her Backing Wind, do you think?' Viking queried, 'but then changed her mind and returned to this new Sunny Intervals of hers?'

'Maybe ...' said Humber, stroking his beard thoughtfully, 'Just maybe ... we should attempt to persuade her to join us ... somehow? She could be very useful you know, now she's been banished from Beaufort.'

'I could spy her out, if you like,' German Bight offered.

Here was a way he could restore their faith in him - and definitely get to be made Second-in-Command.

'Thank you, Bight, but you're needed here to work out that Cabalistic Equation with Hebrides - and I've decided on Malin. You'll be travelling overnight, Malin. Go and get yourself ready, Spy.'

Lundy, appearing with her Atlantic Soup, was just in time to hear Humber's choice. 'How daft sending Malin to spy on a woman!' she giggled. 'Malin knows nothing about the ways of women. He's bound to make a sillybub of hisself. He's such a cold kettle of fish there's no woman I know of yet has managed to thaw 'im out – why, his handshake alone is enough to freeze the 'ow do you do in your throat.'

Nevertheless, Malin-the-Bad packed his personal briefcase (bearing his initials M.T.B. on it – rather a foolish mistake for a spy)… then, after a freezing shower, left inside the darkness of that very night. He hated brightness of any kind, and because the moon was now almost full, he chose to wear black.

Malin enjoyed the punishing cold as he brought under control his choppy team of winds – a new Four-in-hand, Force 8, of Biscay's making. Cleverly, he battled his way through the small Low that Hebrides had formed around Heligoland Hall, behind which they could work on their War Weather.

So, as he sped along, his hands were soon locked rigid with cold around the reins; his face become a dark blue blur; his teeth chattered constantly to themselves - and a fresh set of icicles formed a beard beneath his chin.

By the time he approached Cap Finisterre towards dawn, the skies all around were emptied of a single cloud, and he found himself melting in agony when he suddenly came face to face with the Gulf Stream and its unaccustomed warmth. Then, as dawn broke, the sky was mantled in a soft pink, so Malin slackened his pace, and decided to throw a cold cloak of fog about him for protection.

His Team of Winds reared up when an imposingly-high Cirrus cloud came into view.

Nearer still, Malin detected a mysterious force floating in delicate cob-webby festoons about the fluffy walls of the White Witch's new Residence;

and the tinkling of tiny prisms, he saw, came from pinnacles so tall and thin that their tops shimmered with clashing ice-crystals.

Leaving his team hidden behind a small bank of Cirrostratus to munch at Finisterre's white cloud-lawn – annoyed that they seemed to prefer this to chewing the more wholesome grey cloud at Heligoland - he crept nearer.

Now the walls of the Residence resembled granulated sugar as they slowly turned into pink icing in the fresh glimmers of dawn. Nearer still, he discovered that these were really encrusted with thousands upon thousands of tiny twinkling periwinkles.

As he'd not been invited, the Spy would not ascend the sweeping staircase that rose like a white ribbon towards the front door, but decided instead, to creep carefully round the back.

He edged towards an open window on its Eastern side and, clutching his briefcase tightly for comfort, crouched low beneath its sill, and waited.

The window had been left slightly ajar by Finisterre to let in the early morning breezes to air the rooms. Now her clear trilling voice sang a pretty ditty that issued through the steam of healthy spa-water – a Fair perfume Malin found most distasteful.

The White Witch was in an excellent mood; she'd just decided on a good plan to rescue the Earthling girl and, filled with pleasure at her brilliant idea, was singing a High ditty:

'It's a quarter past Spring and you're late,'
Said the small kippered fish to the Skate.
'You vowed to be here
When Springtime was near.
How could you forget such a date?'

With that she flipped off in great scorn
And decided to marry the Prawn.
But whilst on the way,
She encountered the Cray.
Now they live by the pier at Eastbourne.

Following in the wake of her song, Malin spied an elegant lady, dressed in a seaweedy gown, clustered with quahog clams. She pressed past a row of sponges of colossal bounce and came towards the window where Malin was hiding … noticing that there was a strange Foul smell coming in through the window.

The Spy shot down below the sill, just as the White Witch shut the window above him firmly.

Malin's heart was beating fearfully. But he'd resolved to be brave so, once the catchment window was secured, he peered carefully inside again. He needed to see where the White Witch was going.

Malin was astounded by the magnificence of the bedroom where she now stood. Her floors, he noted, were neatly laid in sea-dredged aggregates, warmed from visible convection currents below; a skilfully-carved oyster bed overloaded with starfish scatter-cushions filled most of the room. Two giant clams hinged together made an admirable bedside chair.

But the lady was already leaving to make her way down a long corridor. Malin leapt from his position – surprised at the ease of doing so, as the warmth had thawed out his knees. Climbing along a ridge of fan-shells, he was soon peering into what must be Finisterre's hall; for a grandfather clock, stating in bold golden letters that it was solar-powered and set to Greenwich Mean Time, ticked merrily away. A display of extraordinary hats and parasols embellished a fish-bone stand; and above this, an array of Victorian samplers celebrated some ancient weather-lore: 'When it thunders, the devil's beating his wife'; 'Make hay while the Sun shines'; and 'Red sky at night, sailors' delight.'

'A Load of cod's wallop!' Malin almost said aloud – but just stopped himself in time - as here was Finisterre, bending to pick up her Rock-Pigeon-Post below her Coat of Arms, which was emblazoned:

'Finisterre Omnia Vincit'

'Mmm, a delightful picture of my brand new self appearing on this week's cover of 'Weather or Not'. How very charming I look.'

She nodded in agreement as she read what it said about her, then frowned as she picked up a second piece of mail. 'Not another Cloud Circular … what does this one promise?

"Take a holiday in the mountains; the clear, rarefied air is recommended for lung disease. Take a holiday in the desert; desert air is clear and dry and beneficial to the heart. Take a sea-cruise; the tonic effect of sea-air is credited with considerable medicinal virtues. Go soon! Go today! Go Now!"

Then the White Witch's expression altered. She felt something not quite right again. That same rather Foul smell was coming in once again from her Hall window. She turned, staring directly towards where Malin watched, transfixed, and walked over to look out.

'She's found me out! Help!' Malin scrambled back round her Residence, leapt over her lumpy cloud-lawn, raced towards his hidden Team of Wind-Forces ... but not quite fast enough.

He'd barely reached his Team before a heaviness such as he'd never known before came upon him. Wraiths of mist entwined his limbs, weaving them into a cocoon of softness as he sank into the gently-yielding lawn. In no time at all he was entranced.

How long he lay there, Malin never knew. But it was long enough for Finisterre to trip down her Cirrostratus steps and stare aghast at her uninvited guest. 'Goodness! What an unlovable face! And what an unfortunate smell he has.'

She searched the initialled briefcase, finding only a few blank papers with Malin-the-Bad's crest: two black sea-monsters strangling one another.

'So, I'm being spied upon, am I? Then I know exactly what to do'.

Finisterre used her wand again, and lightly touched the picture of herself on the cover of 'Weather or Not', which she was still holding. Then she placed the magazine in between the blank Heligoland papers, thus infusing them with LOVE. 'Love – the one emotion those Foul Weather-Makers are incapable of feeling. Yes,' she chuckled, 'I wonder how my little trick turns out? This will be an excellent way into Heligoland Hall to rescue the Earthling.'

But as Finisterre climbed her way back, while half of her was unnaturally excited over her spell, the other half was sunk into gloom. The deed she'd committed was a Foul thing to do – yet she'd enjoyed it immensely. Now she felt one of her 'turns' coming on. 'Oh no! Not again! Not another! Portland Bill will never forgive me!'

Finisterre now found herself extremely emotionally disturbed; her 'other half' was taking advantage of her smallest feelings of weakness. 'Had Portland's Light Therapy been too much … or, indeed, too little?' she wondered.

If she didn't watch out she'd be losing her identity …

A little while later, when Malin came round from his trance, he'd forgotten why he was lying there on the lawn.

But, having now been thoroughly thawed out, he was able to leap onto his Four-in-Hand and blow quickly away.

Imagine his surprise, then, when looking back towards the White Witch's Residence a little while later, he saw the whole place grown overcast; and there, squeezing its way out from a Turret window, a huge black cloud was unfolding.

At first this cloud was ill-formed, its Isobars uncertain. Then, as the thing swirled into an identifiable shape and began to move off in a North-Easterly direction, Malin was able to grin for the first time in his life. What he was witnessing was the formation of a Depression. Though not a large one, it made its way purposefully into the path of the prevailing wind – and strangely – the exact way he was going himself.

Malin knew instinctively which way was North, South, East and West. Wind-Forces never backed or veered under his command.

So, upon reaching the Irish Sea and finding that visibility was practically down to zero with the White Witch's Depression behind and Hebrides' curtain of mist ahead … as an accomplished rider, Malin was able to manoeuvre his Team sideways, increase their speed to that of the prevailing wind… and begin to spiral his way in through the heart of the small Low set around the Castle.

Here, inside the worst of the weather, wild winds seared around his ears, coldness stiffened up his joints, making him feel entirely himself again. Greedily the Low Pressure sucked him in until he landed his great clambering Team on the slimy rocks beneath the ramparts, fretting whether he'd missed breakfast or not.

As he dismounted, Malin slipped and lost control of his briefcase. Horrified, he watched as his precious personal case tumbled through racks of seaweed to sink beneath the waves.

For some time, Malin scrabbled amongst slimy stuff with his cane – but to no avail. In bad temper, he gave up. Flinging his four diminished winds into their stables, he climbed towards the entrance - just as the Foghorn sounded. Every window in the castle had been flung open to let the nourishing fog seep inside.

He strode into the Dining-Hall.

'So, Malin, what have you got to report?'

And Malin, only half way through his Ginger and Whelks, was forced to stand and describe his spying.

'The White Witch, Finisterre, is Fouler than we think,' he announced impressively.

Once the murmurings of delight died down, Humber smiled at this news. 'This intrigues me greatly. Continue with what you've spied.'

Malin eagerly described the Depression squeezing out of the White Witch's Turret window and following him back.

'So, that's where those small Depressions have been coming from,' said Humber. 'Only Weather-Makers from Heligoland know such arts. You know, this particular power of hers must have been inherited as a trait from her Father, Wizard Cromarty.'

'She's undoubtedly become immensely clever – maybe she could even help Bight form our Equation?' suggested Viking, chuckling.

'Yes, yes ... she could be most useful. Well done, Malin; excellent spying indeed ... and what would you like as a reward for this excellent work?'

Malin stroked his icy beard for a moment. He couldn't ask outright to be made Second-in-Command – that would be seen as too grasping. No, he sneered beneath his frozen visage as he made an alternative request:

'To be allowed to evaporate Bight's little Earthling. We were going to evaporate her, remember? She's not needed any longer ... and I do so like evaporating things.'

Lundy, who'd just come in with their Porridge for Pudding, frowned at his request.

'Yes, of course you may. Slime off, Sole. Bring our useless prisoner up ... if she hasn't expired already from the cold.'

While the poor Earthling was being fetched, Biscay bounced to her feet.

'Wait a minute - I've just had a super idea of my very own. Couldn't we get Finisterre here ... by inviting her to Heligoland for a sumptuous meal? She adores food! Then we could really discover whether she's Fair or becoming Foul?'

'Yes, our Lundy's capable of creating a really Foul meal, aren't you, Lundy?' agreed Viking, thumping his breastplate.

Lundy stopped serving Porridge. Her eyes appeared to whirl in their sockets for a while with the exciting thought of cooking a meal for her rival ex-Cordon Bleu Cook from Beaufort. 'I'll not only prepare a meal – I'll create a FEAST!' she announced.

But when the Cook's eyes came to rest on the poor unfortunate Earthling, who entered with Sole, holding up her jeans with her hands ... and now stood trembling to receive her fate ... her large heart began to melt a little with compassion.

'I'll need a lot of help, though, won't I, if I'm to create this Great Feast? It'll take a whole load more of extra work. I'll only carry this out if I can have the little Tome's Guardian for my Helper.'

Wendy, who had no more tears left to shed, and felt quite emptied and without any hope at all, decided to steal round and press closer to her would-be rescuer, while their decision was being made.

She felt safe standing by this huge woman who, out of them all, she considered the most pleasant.

... And, as no-one ever disobeyed Lundy, Humber had to give his permission. 'Yes, yes... of course ... take her away then, as your Helper.'

Lundy was delighted; she loved annoying Malin.

And Malin looked sour. He'd been robbed of his 'little reward', and the Helper had already been pulled quickly inside Lundy's domain. So there was nothing he could do about it. He'd just have to think up something else.

Next to him, Hebrides, too, sat silent, pale and disappointed. She'd heard rumours that the Fair Weather Cook was a skilful temptress; it would be far too dangerous for her GB to be working with this lady on the Equation.

Strange feelings stirred within her. It couldn't be love she felt for him ... Foul Weather-Makers are incapable of love ... no, it was love's first cousin: JEALOUSY: green, possessive, vile. She wanted GB all to herself, to plot with in his dungeon Study forever.

Her eyes blazed the colour of ocean algae as she spun round in her chair and was about to shout out, 'No! This whole Feast idea is preposterous!' when she realized that she would be the one to be shouted down. Better to bide her time.

'I'll go along with the scheme – even assist it a little,' she thought. 'But when the time's ripe, I'll wreck the whole plan; sink it utterly.'

A little later in the day, once Finisterre's Depression was over and the fog blanket alone calmed the bottom of the Irish Sea around Heligoland Hall, a small hermit crab – one of Lundy's – scurried out of the hole where it was hiding. And it spotted among some unnaturally gently-rippling waves, Malin's personal briefcase, which had fallen into the water on his return from spying.

Using its pincers, the small crab managed to undo the catch - meaning to claim this new palace as its own.

Out floated Finisterre's magazine 'Weather or Not' and bobbed to the surface.

German Bight, like Malin, was in a Foul mood, and happened to be pacing the Castle ramparts.

And precisely at that moment, a stray breeze blew by, picked up a lock of German Bight's sea-gelled hair and flopped it down onto his forehead, causing his monocle to fall from his eye and tinkle aimlessly against his chest …

And he was struck … for there, lying slightly out of focus now, was a face on the cover of a glossy magazine bobbing on the waves.

It stared up at him, meeting his gaze, compelling him to rescue it and pick it up. He did so, spellbound by the beauty of its features. The face had flyaway spectacles and a look of great understanding. Then, as he looked, the features appeared to move. The red mouth parted a little. A small salty tear welled in the left eye and trickled down the page ....

And German Bight was smitten. The impossible had happened:

A Foul Weather-Maker had fallen in love.

An unaccustomed warmth crept upwards from his feet, flowed towards his heart and lodged there, enveloping it with all the ecstasies of that Fair Disease.

With his monocle back in, German Bight searched the rest of the picture. The wonderful woman was wearing pink –(suddenly pink became his favourite colour). She stood on the steps of a cloud-cut Residence, a small white Tern clutched to her clam-bespangled breast.

Only then did German Bight see the Coat of Arms above her door: (A hand clutching a roll of ancient weather-maps against a shield of azure upon argent), and a caption below reading: 'Finisterre, White Witch Extraordinaire of Sunny Intervals gives tips on 'How to be Fair'.'

A cry escaped from his lips and fled trembling across the flattened sea. 'Whatever can I do?'

Nothing at all could be done, as, from that moment on, being in the grip of the White Witch's spell, German Bight could only obey its command. For several minutes he stood helpless as a crab without its shell, then … 'No-one must see me with this magazine.'

German Bight hurried back to his Study and instructed his Toad Paperweight to sit on it tight while he attempted to compose himself. He was far too agitated, and quickly locked his door to endure these delicious feelings.

Wendy felt relatively safe at last in front of Lundy's hearth – and was warm for the first time. Lundy fed her some leftover Atlantic Soup, which she'd gulped down eagerly, after which she'd been allowed to rest for a while inside the second largest pan.

She was a little scared of her huge new mistress, but needed to repay her for saving her life. So she decided to work hard - once she'd learned where everything was - and obey the Cook's every command.

When she next awoke, Wendy peered out to see the flattened fish drying from their hooks on the ceiling. They looked like immense swinging doormats, dripping their salty flavours into the Kitchen atmosphere.

Later on, Biscay entered Lundy's domain, holding over one arm, a far more suitable garment for their Earthling girl. She'd created it, using her best blanket-stitch. It was a kind of dungaree with heavy black arrows pointing in every direction.

'Much more suitable for your Kitchen Work,' she said. 'And wearing it won't allow you to forget, Earthling girl, that you are still a POW – a Prisoner of War.'

Wendy put her new garment on. She thought it looked quite trendy as she helped Lundy with her work.

Lundy's Kitchen was enormous; the best kitchen Wendy had ever seen. And she quickly understood that the cold end was where the larder and Deep Freezer were, and the other end, hot. Here, with an open hearth, was where various pots and pans - and what Lundy called skillets - hung from hooks over the flames to spit and sizzle on to the sea-coals below. Peculiar pieces of ship from Hebrides' wrecks steamed on either side. There was always something on the go.

At Supper that evening, German Bight fidgeted on his chair, rather too warm and uncomfortable. Being 'in love' was very difficult: rather like an illness - one that couldn't easily be cured. But he was also still suffering from his vying for the Leadership position once Captain Humber retired - and it was very obvious that this would be offered to Malin now for his excellent spying.

But then, like a stroke of lightning, another moment of sheer genius came to him; one that would trump Malin's spying success with a much more splendid idea of his own.

Yes, Humber's Successor would be himself after all.

'I confess that my fancy has fallen in the White Witch's direction. Could I perhaps even PROPOSE MARRIAGE to her during the visit?'

Never had Bight felt so excessive, never so out of control, so intolerably hot. He clutched at the table for support.

At first shock, then astonishment rippled the length of the table. Sole gave an almighty sneeze; then pandemonium broke out.

'Jolly good show!' whooped Biscay.

'Magnificent!' bellowed Viking.

'What a sacrifice to make for our Castle, Bight,' Humber said, admiringly. 'With this marriage idea of yours – and without the White Witch's help - Beaufort hasn't a chance of winning any kind of War against us now.'

'And I've heard tell that Finisterre loves dancing. We could even have a Celebration Ball,' shouted Viking over the noise.

'I adore dancing!' Sole exclaimed, weeping copiously. She shivered at the thought of enduring a Foul Romance.

Even Malin seemed impressed. Aloud he said, 'I was thinking of having a Ball myself.' Inwardly he thought: 'what a match it'll make. Finisterre, with her obvious beauty and Depressions, will exact a calming influence upon Bight.

Also, in terms of real estate, he won't come off too badly – he'll own all the seaweed and crustaceous crops from the French coast down to the Azores. That detached Cirrostratus Residence, too, could make a grand holiday home – if properly frozen down … Dammit! I should have thought of marrying her myself - that would have been a suitable reward.'

'Sea Scorpions the lot of you!' he wished he could cry aloud.

German Bight retired down to his Study and locked himself in again. After staring at Finisterre's portrait on his 'Weather or Not' magazine until he was thoroughly re-smitten with love, he split open a whole new set of watercolour pencils, then poured himself a cooling glass of Vichy water.

Now he was ready to sit at his capstan desk to compose an invitation to send to the White Witch straight away.

Over a tasteful background of Cowrie pink, he chose Sea-lemon and a few dots of Bladder-wrack brown for the lettering; then shaded the border in Anemone purple with some sweepingly-elegant dashes of Sea-lettuce green. (By the time he'd finished, it looked more like a valentine).

German Bight waited until his heart stopped pounding, then went outside to summon the large Skua from beyond the battlements, commanding it to deliver his Invitation to Sunny Intervals as fast as he could flap.

'You'll be well-rewarded for doing this; you're the biggest and bravest of all my Foul Sea-Birds,' he added … in flattering tones.
(Though he knew that the Foul Weather-Birds were stupid, and didn't realize that Lundy rewarded them purely on whim.)

At Sunny Intervals, Finisterre received a letter marked: 'Urgent. Reply speedily'. It was brought to her by a wretched Great Skua, which dropped the letter from its beak so it clattered onto her sea-dredged aggregate floor. Then it stood at the door, fidgeting rudely on webbed feet, impatient to be off.

'So ill-bred those birds,' remarked Finisterre, pointedly, as she stooped to retrieve the communication.

The heavy envelope was covered in beak-marks, but its contents astonished: it was cut into the shape of a heart and obviously sent by someone in love. 'How very beautiful!'

She consulted her Fair Weather Calendar: February 14th.

'Why, it is St Valentine's Day!'

This information began to stir her deepest feelings of romance. Although the Heligoland Crest advised her of where it came from, she'd noticed some minute lettering hidden in the border: 'GB hoc fecit'

'GB, GB,' she said over and over again. They were different initials from those she'd seen on the briefcase. Her trick of LOVE had obviously worked – but had her magazine, 'Weather or Not' entranced someone else?

The invitation was for two days time. She must on no account accept. It would be a trap; it was bound to be.

As Finisterre paced the hall, her brow grew humid, her heartbeat fluctuated wildly; she blew hot, then blew cold; and all the while, the ugly Skua watched restlessly, ruffling his feathers, which he then proceeded to preen in the rudest of fashions.

'Tell them I'm unable to go,' she decided.

'Yes, I accept,' Fitzroy contradicted in a gruffer voice, intruding from within her.

The Skua squinted at the White Witch in confusion.

'No we don't,' Finisterre insisted.

'We accept with pleasure,' Fitzroy insisted louder, making her scribble a quick acceptance.

The Skua cleared off with that reply. 'Using the Royal 'We' are we now?' He cracked harshly as he flew back fast to Heligoland Hall - expecting a huge reward from the Cook.

The Skua failed to see, below him, what he should have spotted: a dark blanket of oil, seeping slowly along on the calm sea's surface. But the reply, carried in his beak, prevented him from looking anywhere but straight ahead.

He did, however, deliver Finisterre's acceptance in record time ... but cleared off, mightily offended, when Lundy only offered him leftover Bird's Custard.

'Now that the White Witch has graciously agreed to come to our Feast,' Humber announced the following morning, 'we'll have to make the Castle acceptable. Such an important guest shouldn't be alarmed in any way. There's to be no Foul War-Weather at all for the time being. For the moment she arrives, the Castle must be calm … and Heligoland Hall … thoroughly cleaned.'

A jolt of shock rippled through every Foul Weather-Maker; Their Castle had never been cleaned.

'Hebrides, you'll dispel the gloom; Biscay flatten the waves; Sole, you must overcome your natural inclinations and use de-mister; and Malin, an-tifreeze … though you can keep the cold air-conditioning on in your rooms. Viking, you have to apply strong detergent to the Castle walls and remove all traces of limpet and sea-slime from the battlements … so that on her arrival, the Lady won't slip over.

As for you, Lundy and Windy, you'll scour both the insides - and outsides of your pans - in case, being a cook herself, the White Witch desires to inspect the Kitchen.'

Lundy was outraged. Yes, cook a Feast she would – a magnificent one – ideas were already forming in her mind: Finisterre would be quite drowned in the glory of her Bouillabaisse Soup … but to clean her pans was unbearable; it would ruin the flavour. 'Come on, Windy!' she said, making a thunderous exit, and slamming the Kitchen door.

Captain Humber felt weary and old; he couldn't control his Cook's tantrums as he used to - and a little more of him evaporated.

As for German Bight, he was confined to his Study to continue working on the Cabalistic Equation. Hebrides would join him once she'd dispelled the gloom.

'The White Witch should at least see you've made an effort – if we're to persuade her to join us to help complete this important Equation,' said Humber.

Lundy (and Wendy) sang lustily as they went about their work and, before long, Wendy was intimate with several Foul Ditties, which she found she rather enjoyed singing.

By the end of the morning, fed up with continually being drilled and sent out to patrol calm seas, the Foul Weather-Birds returned and clamoured for rewards outside the Kitchen window.

Lundy took full advantage of the situation: whilst feeding the Foul Birds dainty leftover gobbets of food with one hand, to please them, she grabbed a couple of feet with the other …

'but only after they've eaten, Windy', she instructed. 'Let'em get stuffed first, then we needn't bother later. After that, hang'em in the Heligoland Deep Freezer by their two webbed feet thus, so's the 'little stiffs' can stretch out and harden a little for a week or two, 'til they're ready for when you want'em.'

'Yes, Lundy,' said Wendy, politely. She was learning fast.

Lundy went to bed that night to dream about preparations for her mighty feast the following day.

Wendy was about to go to sleep herself - on her new Gulls' feather mattress inside the second largest pan.

All day long as she happily polished and brightened the outsides of every copper pan in the Kitchen, she'd caught a few glimpses of her own reflection. A strange look had crept into her eyes; her hair was irretrievably tangled into an unruly bird-nest shape.

Staring longer at this reflection, she wondered what was happening to her… something was: her whole face had altered in a strange way.

'I think I'm turning Foul,' she whispered to the wild face that stared back at her. Maybe it's the different atmosphere here in Heligoland? Or probably its all this Foul food I'm eating?'

Part 4
Witches' War

Chapter 14
Pink Champagne

Finisterre left Sunny Intervals on her Backing Wind. This had been invigorated from munching on her new cloud-lawn, and now was so choppy that she needed to rein it in. For she had to ride sidesaddle … and slowly … because of her wonderful dress.

Beside her, she had, on short rein, a second Wind-Force. This was labouring under two full crates of vintage wine: one a delicate pink champagne, the other a superb dessert wine from Chateau d'Yquem. Both had been infused by her with such a subtle magic that they gleamed like galaxies on a star-lit night.

Finisterre travelled easily through empty skies. She'd gathered from the Shipping Forecast that morning that the weather around Heligoland was *Fair: force 2, 4 miles, good* - so she was in High spirits and recited to herself her favourite Shakespearean ditty:

'Out upon it! I have loved
Three whole days together,
And am like to love three more
If it prove Fair Weather'

Towards the end of the morning, however, she faltered, growing scared. They'd just passed over an enormous blanket of blackness, creeping slowly and purposefully exactly the way they were going themselves.

'Goodness!' she remarked.

'Good!' Fitzroy remarked, deep within her.

Finisterre fished out her Rescue Remedy and took a few more drops to keep him down; she did not want Fitzroy interfering in her plans for the day.

Then, later, when they'd reached the middle of the Irish Sea, there it was before them – the Foul Castle itself.

Finisterre found herself shimmering with unexpected excitement. Every-where around her was as calm as untroubled custard. Where were the Sea-Serpents? Where all the slime? The barnacles? … the Low she'd been led to believe surrounded Heligoland Hall?

Instead, a pale silver moon still hung there in full daylight. It threw a gentle streak of rippling light across the water where she was to land. Finisterre curved her Wind-Forces downwards, greatly touched at the obvious flattening of the waves especially for her.

'How courteous of them,' she thought.

Inside Heligoland Hall, things were not quite so calm.

Only German Bight was in raptures – knowing that he was to 'propose'. Because of this, he'd been given the privilege of escorting the White Witch upon her arrival, and was immaculately dressed as usual.

Hebrides, however, was nervous. She needed to look her very best in front of her rival. Changing from her usual wrecking-clothes, she'd slipped into a gorgeous seaweedy gown, dyed green with the juice of spirogyra to a special shade she called Shagreen. This kicked up behind her, after slithering over her marvellous figure to stop just short of her lethal black boots.

'What can I do to look smart?' wondered Wendy, seeing how German Bight and Hebrides looked for their important guest.

Then, on an impulse, she grabbed the Kitchen scissors and slashed each of her own dungaree trouser-bottoms into a pointed fringe as high up as she dared. 'That's better … far more modern,' she thought.

Captain Humber wore his usual 'Gansey' Fisherman's knit; Biscay shed her mac - but left her headscarf on; Viking – a little excessively - put on his best armour … even Lundy wore a large clean apron.

Only the dismal Sole dithered, wringing her hands, not ready in time.

'Get yourself into a party dress, quick, Sole,' Hebrides ordered. 'You look worse than one of my wrecks.'

Sole was scared of the Black Witch: she didn't like the way her eyes flashed around. Somewhat dampened in spirits, she slid quickly to her room.

Taking a quick gulp from her vat of boiling cough mixture, she wafted through the usual Kitchen steam seeping through the crack in her chimney, and gained the courage to search her wardrobe for a suitable unaired dress. Easing this on, she waded through her Post-it notes up to the mirror, where she brushed her hair in a half-hearted way … until her reflection misted up completely and she could no longer see her face with its red-rimmed eyes. She was ready.

91

While her Wind Forces were being stabled by Biscay, Finisterre was greeted on the ramparts by a handsome man wearing an impeccable dinner-jacket. He looked terribly smitten. 'GB?' she dared enquire.

'Yes, indeed. Allow me,' he replied, ushering the Fair Lady through the front door. Overflowing with emotion, he led her along the corridor, past a special Art Exhibition of 'Dead Life' put on by Biscay, and another of 'Recently-wrecked and dried Ship-Pieces' by Hebrides, and on into the Dining Hall.

Finisterre noticed a distinct soapy smell everywhere, but said nothing. She behaved like the Guest of Honour she was supposed to be.

There was a gasp as Finisterre, the White Witch, entered the Dining Hall on German Bight's trembling arm. The atmosphere around her was electric. Her hair, arranged in a hundred serpentine curls, had each curl held in place with a blushing clam. Her lips, outlined in a cupid's bow, were stung with 'Starfish Red' to make them full – and to match her fingernails. Her dress clung to her body in an alarmingly provocative way, which caused German Bight's teeth to clench; for it fell in one sky-blue sweep from her shoulders, fanning at the hem to resemble a fish's tail. In her hand she clutched a smart bag, constructed from tiny fan-shells neatly hinged together.

As she was escorted to her place, the 'Aurora Borealis' polish on her shoes left pools of quicksilver wherever she trod.

Only Hebrides glared at her rival. Her garment now shimmered jealously against her sides. A last-minute alteration in her dress showed the hem daringly raised with a crab-pincer, to reveal a pair of black fishnet stockings above her boots.

Deftly, German Bight removed his Lady's seaweed wrap (which swelled protectively round her when it rained, but shrank to almost nothing when Fine), and settled the elegant lady into her seat.

'How delightful you look, my dear,' he murmured into her ear … adding something about 'being seasoned with mellow fruitfulness' … which confused Finisterre to blush.

The White Witch's two crates were presented to Lundy, who performed a kind of curtsey as she took them to cool down for a moment or two in the Heligoland Deep Freezer.

'I now declare this Feast open,' Humber announced. He hoped fervently that the White Witch would be impressed.

Biscay jumped up to say Grace … but two hands pulled her down roughly … it would have been 'Bad Form' to read Foul poetry on so auspicious an occasion.

To avoid embarrassment, Viking leapt to his feet and cranked down a huge net of Hors D'oeuvres, which hung unsteadily from the candelabra, being overburdened with countless crustaceous titbits, garnished with bait and Arbroath Smokies.

This fell the last few feet with a crash, sending its delicious contents onto everyone's plates. With loud clapping, the Feast had begun.

Nobody noticed the Barometer begin to rise as the pressure rose.

Nobody noticed the temperature at Heligoland Hall climb high as that of Beaufort … with added humidity from Lundy's cauldron of Bouillabaisse soup, which she wheeled in to suffuse the air with a myriad reekings from the depth of the Irish Sea.

Wendy was allowed to serve this course using Lundy's ladle.

Finisterre was relieved to see the Earthling girl no longer in the damp dungeon … but shocked at the wild state of her, realizing that she'd have to be rescued very quickly … or was it already far too late?

It was during this course, in a series of loud reports, that corks flew up from Finisterre's pink champagne.

Alerted by the barrage, the White Witch whispered a spell under her breath to activate the magic … while flagons of her champagne were circulated:

'Awake all secret passions and grow warm;
From Foulest hate to lusty love be born.
Cause deep desires to dwell where none before;
And let sweet music change the face of War.'

The Foul Weather-Makers had never tasted champagne.

Bubbles fizzed in Humber's beard, caused Lundy's eyes to whirl, producing uncontrollable giggling in Biscay. Viking filled his drinking-horn to the brim and drained it in one gulp, beating his armoured chest like a demon possessed, so powerful were the fumes.

Sole wept with pleasure, thus over-salting her soup.

Even Wendy sneaked a large sip from Lundy's glass in the Kitchen, taking advantage of the Cook, now swaying as she sang a sea-shanty while serving her fish course next door: Moray Eels steamed in their jackets.

These stretched side by side, with heads one end of the table, tails the other. They reclined on the most dignified Spode Eel dishes. Not once, in all her Cordon Bleu days, had Finisterre been so impressed.

But this was the moment she needed to murmur:

'Love among the Fair brings happiness and joy.
Love among the Foul will weaken, then destroy.'

As glasses were raised and drunk, her spell began to take effect. Everyone looked flushed, a few passionate, some even happy. Laughter filled the Hall; steam rose from Sole's napkin. The Barometer climbed still higher.

In the Kitchen, Wendy's head felt fizzy as she stole a second sip of the wonderful stuff …

And it was while collecting fishplates from the table that she stared at Finisterre. Suddenly she was struck. Never had she seen such a wonderful woman. 'I will try to be exactly like her when I'm older,' she promised, brushing back her unruly hair.

But Finisterre herself had made one tragic mistake: she'd forgotten her own intolerance to champagne; it was going straight to her head. It would've been most impolite (and maybe a little suspect) for her not to drink some of the gift as well. She leaned further across the table to fix her eyes on German Bight. ' "GB hoc fecit",' she whispered, quoting from the invite. He was extremely handsome: his aquiline face had a look of evil tinged with intelligence. Like his figure, his hands were long, refined and aristocratic – she loved that. A man of such elegance and taste must be no less than a Count.

'Countess Bight,' she murmured. The title thrilled her.

In response, German Bight's passion rose parallel with the Barometer. Eagerly he searched for her hand beneath the table, but found Sole's clammy one instead. Its dampness sent a shiver of repulsion up his arm. But once he had grasped her hand, German Bight felt that to let go might offend the lady, who looked surprised enough as it was; no man had ever held her hand.

Sole was just beginning to wonder if she liked it or not, when both Hebrides

94

and Finisterre, looking across the table, saw the Doleful One lift her hand entwined with German Bight's slightly above the table, and both discovered what was going on.

Finisterre was at once smitten with a new Foul passion. Pangs of jealousy she'd never felt before. And, inside her, Fitzroy found himself being aroused with feelings of desire for the Black Witch - a new unusual passion he'd never felt before - that of Fair love.

Hebrides was confused. She was relieved to find it was not the White Witch's hand that her GB sought – but Sole's.

However, something not quite right was going on. Why were the White Witch's eyes drilling into hers, filled with both jealousy - and love? How was that possible?

She needed to think about it urgently. 'Could it be something to do with that woman's gift to us perhaps ... the drink maybe?' Sensibly, she'd hardly touched a drop.

Quietly, she excused herself, and went to her room.

Sole was forced to withdraw her hand when she was called to the Kitchen to help slide an enormous slippery Octopus to rest comfortably on its oval dish. But feelings of desire, experienced for the first time in her life, soon vanished, as she realized she could never have German Bight. It was Finisterre ... or was it still Hebrides whom he desired?

In either case, her new love would be unrequited; she'd suffer most terribly.

The main course, the Octopus, was hauled to the centre of the table, where its two eyes stared resentfully at everyone around.

'Windy, spread the tentacles out in rays, the tips of which have got to reach everybody's plate,' Humber called out in a drunken state.

Each person was obliged to nibble a tentacle until it ended. Then the central body was ripped open to reveal its stuffing – a host of Pilchards in a gravy of ginger and Whelks.

Throughout this course, Biscay thrilled as she watched Malin's face gradually thawing. Leaning towards him, she dared say, 'You've jolly good features, you know, underneath all that ice. You should thaw out more often.' Then Biscay trilled in a gust of wind at her own joke. She would enjoy being in love.

Lundy finished Hebrides' glass of champagne in the Kitchen, then wheeled in the salad course jauntily. Her Ocean Salad was composed of a single savagely-frayed Sea-cabbage, the heart of which had been torn out, to be replaced with Sea-gooseberries, Sea-squirts and Sprats. The whole had been drenched with Windy's own grey concoction of Sea-slug and Plankton sauce … and was now so tasty, that Heinz, by mixing together all 57 varieties, could not have done better.

The Cook stared at Viking, surveying with wonder his muscles bulging around his breastplate.

She served him tenderly, giving him the largest portion.

Sudden vibrations shivered the surface of the final course: a Jellyfish Blancmange encrusted with gaudy polyps. But nobody really trusted Lundy's desserts any more, and Humber gestured Wendy to quickly wheel it out into the kitchen again.

Viking was winding up his ancient gramophone to tempt people into the Ballroom next door.

Only Humber was left behind.

Unnoticed by anyone, he'd slid beneath the table. There, he'd fallen in love once again with his dead wife, Shannon.

'It's only you I love,' he whispered to her ghost.

Chapter 15

Sweet Music and Fair Love

German Bight arose and, escorting his Lady to the Ballroom, wafted her eagerly to the centre of the room to waltz her deftly around.

'This is my favourite: *Singing in the Rain*', she whispered breathlessly.

Biscay pulled Malin from his chair, inviting him to dance and, as his knees had thawed out, he could hardly refuse. Fox-trotting to *Blow, blow thou winter's wind* caused Biscay's new Foulard scarf to collapse into folds around her neck as he danced her jerkily around.

But why wasn't he responding? A hurtfulness spread through her; his eyes were focused on somewhere far beyond. The object of his love wasn't her at all. Detaching herself, she fled to her room to try to endure this weird new feeling of love and come to terms with it.

Lundy deserted Windy, who was still quietly tasting some of the delicious blancmange in the Kitchen, in order to fling herself into Viking's reciprocating arms. 'What's happening to me? My heart's leapin' like a Porpoise!', she whooped as they galloped around, her ladle clanging urgently against his armour.

'You're the only woman who can withstand my embrace,' he bellowed, responding by whirling her to the strains of Stormy Weather. But his sharp Nordic helmet horns were so lethal, that soon the floor was theirs alone.

Once this selfish couple was eventually persuaded to leave the Ballroom, they went to watch a sinking Sun play upon the beauty of the Heligoland sea. Viking, armour and all, plunged into the flattened waves to cool himself down, while Lundy waited patiently on the shore. Then, by extending her ladle, she helped him to land, leading him back to her Kitchen, where they toppled over into the great Heligoland sugar-bin.

Wendy, alarmed at the approach of this disturbingly large couple, fled out onto the ramparts where, taking her backpack to sit on, she stared at the sea, thinking about the wonderful White Witch, Finisterre.

In the Ballroom, Sole, tired of waiting for a lover who never appeared, decided to go it alone, leaving a slime-trail behind her.

Only German Bight and Finisterre were able to elegantly pirouette on Sole's slime, until even they could stand it no longer.

Taking this opportunity, German Bight lured his partner down the stone stairway into his dungeon Study. The time had arrived for him to propose.

Poor Sole was left spinning sadly round to Raindrops keep Falling on my Head … until the ancient gramophone stuck in a single track, and she was caught, mesmerized, sailing round and round like a skater in an icy groove.

German Bight's Study had not been cleaned, and the unusual heat, rushing to fill this colder dungeon, condensed rapidly on the steps. Finisterre felt compelled to clutch German Bight's hand. This caused his eye-glass to steam up.

Missing the bottom step, he fell heavily sideways into her arms.

In response, Finisterre's own glasses misted over. Unable to see, she found that she had leant forwards straight onto German Bight's lips. In this embrace, fog, steam and heat arose, mingling all around, enveloping them entirely.

'Foulest treasure, live a life of sin with me. Come over to our side. Be bad with me,' he entreated, tightening his arms around her waist.

'Oh yes,' Fitzroy responded, with a soft, vulnerable voice inside her.

'It can never be,' Finisterre contradicted. 'Alas, I am too Fair.' But her heart was supersaturated with desire, and she recalled her Coat of Arms: *Amor Omnia Vincit – Love Conquers All.*

'Fairest Foul,' German Bight persisted, 'did they not expel you from Beaufort?'

'Yes,' replied Finisterre, sadly.

'Yes, indeed,' reiterated Fitzroy, his voice gradually gaining in confidence.

'And sometimes, don't you feel deeply depressed?'

'Yes I do!' answered Finisterre and Fitzroy together.

Once again, they were overcome with a terrible weakness as they drew together and sank to the Study floor.

Finisterre shuddered with unusual delight. She'd never felt so wicked; it was glorious.

Eventually, German Bight overheated, and had to disengage himself. With a dramatic gesture, he flung his arms to encompass his whole Study: 'My capstan table, hurricane lamp, globe – even my Toad Paperweight … all this will be yours – and more. Together we'll defeat the Fair Weather-Makers; together plunge the British Isles into permanent freezing weather …'

'How?' asked Fitzroy eagerly as Finisterre sat in German Bight's lap on the bottom step.

'Well, we've captured the book of Cabalistic signs from Earth. With this, we'll form an Equation, allowing us to wage war on Beaufort.
When we've won, I'll rule Heligoland, and YOU will be my Queen. Help us overcome Britain, blasting them with sleet and snow. Help us evaporate Faeroes, Fastnet, Plymouth, Fisher …'

'N… No!' stammered Finisterre, coming to her senses … 'not Fisher.'

In anguish, she held herself back from the entreaties, and suddenly sat on the globe, which began to revolve. Her head and Fitzroy spun one way, her heart and Finisterre the other …

'Fisher, GB. Fisher, GB
Who shall it be? Who shall it be?'

But German Bight was down on one knee, attempting to grab Finisterre's hand as it spun around the world. The globe stopped with a grinding wrench. Her hand was unbearably warm, but as he pressed it to his lips, he implored, 'Foulest Fair, I offer you my undying affection and total services in all Meteorological Matters … and beg you to marry me.'

It was a magnificent proposal; she'd never have such an offer again. He was so handsome, so indisputably charming.

Finisterre wavered only for an instant … an instant in which her soul cried out for a life of sin; her heart was melting.

But then, as German Bight drew her down for a second time, she saw, written clearly on the blackboard behind him, some advanced mathematical sums.

'That's it – the Cabalistic Equation!'

Instantly, Finisterre captured the valuable information, employing her photographic memory. A large black book lay below it, which had inscribed on its cover 'Cabalistic Weather-signs and symbols' by Johann Heinrich Lambert.

'Yes. Yes. Yes.' cried Fitzroy … while Finisterre's mind was elsewhere.

'NO! NO! NO!' shrieked another, higher voice.

There, at the Study door, loomed the Black Witch, green, omnipotent, vile. 'You shall not have him! German Bight is MINE!'

As Hebrides descended step by step, German Bight, down on one knee, quickly gathered his dazed senses and, leaning forwards, endeavoured to trip her up on the last step.

'Oh no you don't! You'll stay just where you are: down on one knee – but to ME not to her.' And with that, the Black Witch crackled some bony fingers, throwing a strong electro-magnetic field around him, beyond which he could not pass.

Finisterre, initially confused, was struck by the current's searing force, and stepped back from German Bight in the nick of time.

Turning her back to the Black Witch, she searched her top pocket frantically for her Attire-of-Sea-Pinks Rescue Remedy.

'And you'll stay down here, too.' Hebrides directed her fingers towards her rival.

But Finisterre spun round and flung the phial sharply like a grenade at the Black Witch's feet. The phial shattered into fragments, sending out a heavy burst of Fine Perfume.

Hebrides doubled over, choking and gasping on the Fair poison, giving Finisterre enough time to grab the Tome (which immediately turned golden), raise up her dress, lunge up the stairs, and fly past her into the Hall.

'Don't leave me, Finisterre!' called German Bight, pitifully.

But Finisterre had gulped in some fumes of her own Remedy as she dashed past, - and it was enough to completely clear her head. Rescue – that was the reason she'd accepted their invitation - Rescue the Earthling. Destroy the Tome - exactly as Portland Bill had directed … 'before I foolishly became the victim of my own Spell of Love.'

Out on to the rocks, the White Witch ran. There she saw Wendy sitting rather forlornly, overlooking the flattened Irish Sea.

'Quick, Earthling child, guard this Tome inside your backpack and keep yourself hidden while I fetch my two Wind-Forces. You and the Tome are coming with me. Where are the Stables?'

Wendy jumped up joyfully to see her idol advancing. 'I don't know where they are; they haven't let me go Wind-riding yet. I've never even been out here before. But I'd like to come with you very much.' Wendy was impressed; the Lovely lady wanted her … and she'd found the Tome – although it was now turned golden. But Wendy was wise to its ways and quickly hid it in her backpack as it returned to green.

Finisterre, following her intuition, made off over the rocks below the ramparts. Yes, she'd guessed the way correctly. There, beyond the ramparts, was a passageway leading to the Central Courtyard and the Stables.

But there also, in front of where her Wind Forces were stalled, was the Black Witch, standing with boots astride and arms crossed over her chest.

'No-one, not even you, White Witch, escapes past me!' she shrieked, fixing Finisterre with narrowed eyes. And she drew an ebony wand from one of her high-heeled boots.

In response, Finisterre hoisted her skirts still higher, and fished out the new powerful wand from the top of her suspender belt.

Now the two Witches faced one another, and the fighting began in earnest. Spells were hurled; electricity streaked across the battlements, bouncing from one wall to the next.

Wendy crouched behind a rock away from the line of fire. She was terrified – yet exhilarated. Nothing had been anything like this in her whole life.

Hebrides flashed from green to black to scarlet, choosing her Force. Eventually, she felt comfortable with Infra-red.

Finisterre responded with Ultra-violet.

Soon, a full electric storm was raging.

Blue and red rays ricocheted off windows like reflections in a firework display. The Barometer in the Hall climbed and fell, climbed and fell, confusing its mercury interior until it exploded.

Among the Heligoland chimneys, discharged shocks sprang from pot to pot. Uncertain, the Weather-Vane spun giddily around. Wendy was almost knocked backwards by the Force. She crouched lower still.

Now Hebrides was battling from a dominant position on the rampart walls, her prickly current about to overpower the White Witch below … Yes, she almost had her … but what was happening? Suddenly there seemed to be two people for her to fight.

The Fitzroy part of the White Witch was coming to the fore, changing from her into a more masculine form! Was this White Witch somehow able to summon extra assistance by splitting like this? Hebrides staggered backwards, confused. The White Witch had cleverly severed herself: one half of her enemy was fighting against her, the other being drawn nearer with arms outstretched - and she found herself strangely drawn to this other part of the White Witch.

Hebrides shuddered; this situation was impossible. She'd have to summon extra help herself. Lifting her head skyward, she emitted a fearful sailors' whistle; a weird, summoning call, which penetrated high as the Castle Turrets, low as the bed of the Irish Sea.

In answer to her command, Toads tumbled from the ramparts, Sea-Serpents slithered with difficulty up soapy battlement walls, Ship-Rats raced over rocks to surround her enemy. Wendy stood up from her hiding-place screaming in terror at the creatures.

'Wendy!' Finisterre yelled. 'Fetch the two Fair Wind-Forces from the Stables. Hurry!'

The Fitzroy part of her was eagerly pushing Finisterre's body in front of him in his image, travelling safely through ranks of vile screeching Ship-Rats, squirms of hissing Sea-Serpents … finally clambering up the ramparts past hoards of croaking Toads, towards the Black Witch … and certain defeat.

Hebrides was astounded. How could the White Witch do this? And how could she walk so fearlessly through her Foul army of creatures? This Witch was far stronger than she imagined, appearing to be totally unaffected by the extra help. She gave a howl of rage, which only excited Fitzroy to a greater pitch … he liked a little rage in a woman.

With one final, frantic attempt to stop this dual approach, Hebrides sharpened the rocks to razor-points beneath the White Witch's feet.

But here was Wendy, leading out one Wind-Force. She'd not managed to encourage Finisterre's other Fair Wind to go with her: it had refused to let the strange Earthling handle it.

Finisterre was using all her remaining energy to wrench Fitzroy's gaze away from the Black Witch and pull him back into herself.

Once accomplished, this allowed her to spring lightly from one sharpened rock to the other on crystal-soled eel-skin shoes towards her Backing Wind.

Realizing Finisterre was about to escape, Hebrides leapt from the battlements and, taking a deep breath, hurled towards the White Witch the Foulest curses she could muster.

Now it was Finisterre's time to cringe. Never had she heard anything so appalling.

But then, to Finisterre's surprise, coming out of her own Fair lips – but in Fitzroy's lower key - she heard language even Fouler. She pressed her hands over her ears to shield what was issuing from her own mouth … realizing at the same time, that if she were ever to escape with the Earthling, she'd have to put Fitzroy from her once and for all … sever him completely … leave Heligoland without him.

Wendy cringed as well. She was not used to such Foul language, and Finisterre's strange masculine voice both horrified and thrilled her. But she remembered the Tome, and quickly picked up her backpack before leading the Backing Wind out over the rocks, ready to give to the White Witch to escape on.

But where was the second Wind-Force? Why had the Earthling brought out only one?

'Mount the Backing Wind, quickly, Wendy!' Finisterre yelled.

Wendy had never ridden anything before – except her bike, but dutifully swung herself on to the frightened creature and pointed it towards Finisterre, flew it over the sharply-pointed rocks, to allow the White Witch to mount the Wind-Force and blow safely away.

Hebrides saw the Earthling about to help the White Witch leave, and did some speedy lateral thinking. 'Wasn't the White Witch a cook? Then maybe there was just one final piece of ammunition she could fling at her … something so lethal to a Fair Weather cook that …'

And she took action FAST. With a few well-chosen Abracadabras, she smothered Finisterre with a poisonous cloud of yellow sulphurous smoke.

The smell of stinking bad eggs was a final blow to Finisterre. It offended all her culinary senses. She gave a desperate gasp, collapsed to her knees, floundering like one of the Black Witch's own capsizing ships.

But the sulphur smell acted like the crack of a sharp whip to her Backing Wind. The Wind Force suddenly shied, and leapt into the air. Then, with her last spark of energy, Finisterre directed her wand towards it. 'Home!' she ordered. 'Fly back home!'

'This Wind Force is for you to escape on!' screamed Wendy.

She was now scared of her idol's new double appearance … and wasn't quite sure she wanted to escape with this apparition after all.

Her pleas were in vain. She tried to dismount, but the Wind-Force did as her Mistress bid. Already it was curving upwards in a smooth sweeping arc away from the Castle and the dreadful sulphur fumes – with Wendy frantically clinging on, still protesting loudly.

Triumphant and cackling with laughter, the Black Witch showered Finisterre (Fitzroy appeared to enjoy the smell, and was showing his presence once more) with wave after wave of static electricity, until the two became one again and could no longer move

Finally, the static blacked Finisterre out completely.

The White Witch was hers.

Chapter 16
The Big Sleep

Hebrides sank to her knees, exhausted; weak as the underneath of a rusting wreck. With her power used up, her feeling of triumph over the White Witch did not last.

'She's really triumphed over me,' she thought, 'sending Windy off to warn Beaufort, instead of escaping herself. Why, oh why didn't I destroy the Earthling Girl first?'

And now she found herself in a terrible situation: if the others discovered she'd let the Earthling get back to Sunny Intervals, and that word was bound to reach Beaufort, alerting them of what had happened, and warning them of War - then every inhabitant of Heligoland would turn against her. She, herself, could be evaporated.

But although her wand was spent, Hebrides could at least do one thing: put her two lips together and blow.

There was an immediate response from the skies. The entire Flock of Foul Weather-Birds obeyed the Black Witch and came hurtling down, crying loudly.

'Bring me back that Earthling! There'll be rewards for you all! For if you don't succeed, I warn you: you'll soon be Fighting for your very Feathers … for there's bound to be War!'

In a winged explosion, the whole flock rose up to give chase, circling once or twice to get their bearings, then swerving off in a dense black cloud.

Hebrides' victory was further diminished when, going back inside, she soon discovered their valuable Tome was missing ... 'That Earthling must've taken it … yes … it must've been in that backpack of hers; it looked heavy enough. And without it – how can Bight and I finish the Equation? Once it's in Beaufort's hands, they'll use it for their own ends. No, the other Foul -Weather-Makers will certainly destroy me.'

Her dismay only deepened when she found that every one of the Foul Weather-Makers was still spellbound; continuing to behave like complete idiots, trapped inside the White Witch's Love potion …

Hebrides made her way despondently to Lundy's Kitchen. First she sniffed the remains of Lundy's glass of Pink Champagne. 'Yes, this was a strong Love Potion, just as I suspected.'

Then her eyes came to rest on the second crate, placed unopened on top of the Heligoland Freezer.

Opening one of the bottles of Chateau d'Yquem, she sniffed more deeply into its neck - and immediately yawned heavily. A strong Sleeping Draught must have been mixed into it, she realized.

'So that's what she was going to have us drink next! She would then be able to finally subdue us all with this stuff! Then I'll use it myself to good effect,' she smiled with relief … 'that is … until I can regenerate my strength.'

Making her way around the castle to each inhabitant - starting with the two she discovered rumbling behind her in the sugar-bin - Hebrides prized open their mouths and gave every one of them a large desert-spoonful.

But when Hebrides went down to deal with German Bight, she discovered him sobbing pathetically on the floor of his Study. He was crouched over something clutched tightly to his chest. He looked in a deplorable state. Several bottles of Vichy water lay around his feet where he'd drunk himself to saturation point.

Hebrides attempted to grab the magazine that GB clutched to himself. He would not let her take it away.

Then she gave a start: it was a Fair magazine called 'Weather or Not', with Finisterre's face upon the cover. 'How could you be tricked like that? Traitor! Deceiver!' Hebrides forced open GB's mouth and dosed him, too. 'You'll sleep like all the rest then. And I'll lock you inside your dungeon Study. It's only for your own good!'

The sleeping draught had immediate effect on each love-stricken inmate. Going up to their rooms, they soon collapsed senseless onto their beds –

All except for Malin, whom she dosed as he lay moribund outside the true object of his love: the Master Bedroom, which, by rights, he thought, would soon be his. It faced North, so enjoyed the severest weather conditions, since it was in the path of every gale that hit the Castle.

Finally, the weary Black Witch dosed her overpowered opponent, the collapsed White Witch, whose body she dragged with difficulty into the dungeon. Taking her wand away, she locked the door securely.

'No-one must know about any of this – or there'll be hell to pay.'

When, later, the Flock had still not returned with the Earthling, Hebrides knew that Victory had definitely been won by Finisterre. However, Hebrides also knew that now she was the only one who could save Heligoland Hall.
'With our whole castle trapped and inflicted with that White Witch's disease, which I, the Black Witch, have no energy left to dispel - and with both wands and magic completely spent, there's only one possible option.'

Hastily, she slipped from the castle to rest and recover her powers down on Earth, in Foulness Point on the South-East coast of England.

In the mild, perfect weather, Wendy's Backing Wind was able to blow as hard as it could, upwards from Heligoland and into the evening sky. Her head still spun with terrible oaths and frightening Witches' sparks.

Then, all at once, Wendy found she was exultant ... 'I am actually riding the Wind! I've always dreamed of doing exactly this,' she laughed.

The wind was in her hair, brushing against her face, the sun going down in the West. It was utterly fabulous ...

... Until she heard screeching below and saw a huge flock of Foul Sea- Birds coming after her.

'Hurry! Hurry!' she urged the poor Backing Wind. The flock was gaining on them - fast.

Finisterre's Wind tried her best, ascending rapidly through the blue. But the higher Wendy flew, the further upwards the Sea-Birds flew after her, screaming Foul abuse ... which she was now perfectly able to understand.

And they'd re-arranged themselves into Biscay's well-trained V-formation, closing off any escape sideways, pushing Wendy vertically, higher and higher, with one wave after another taking turns at the front. Eventually, they gained the Cirrostratus.

Never had Wendy been so high up. She started to pant as the oxygen decreased, thinned out, and practically disappeared.

Still the Sea-Birds funneled up, the fiercest forming the apex.

Then, above the Cirrostratus, the heavier Cormorants and Shags dropped back one by one through lack of air, leaving the remainder in a tightly-packed spiral, wheeling and crying immediately below.

Wendy was now gasping for breath. She clung on for all she was worth, urging her Wind Force to climb still higher.

But gaping beaks had reached her, scissoring at her with sharp, agonizing pecks. Wendy fought them off, trying to smash them down with her feet. But they grabbed her already-slashed dungaree, clawing at the frayed edges, ripping them to finer shreds, gashing her legs, taunting her, trying to force her from her steed.

Then a very strange thing happened. Wendy suddenly found herself wrenched sideways into a strong, swiftly-flowing current of air. To her surprise, she was flying faster and easier than before.

In no time at all, the funnel of birds dwindled to a thin ribbon way behind.

Wendy couldn't believe her luck.

She had found and climbed into the Jet Stream.

Accustoming herself to the diminished pressure and feeling of breathlessness took Wendy a while. But she found she could cope with this new pressure, provided she breathed in short fast gasps.

And the Jet Stream was helpful too. Not only had it carried her from danger; it was now taking her with great efficiency in the dark – not towards Finisterre's Sunny Intervals Residence – but flowing directly towards the Wind-Forces previous home ... first The Bristol Channel - then Beaufort Castle.

Chapter 17
Crash Landing at Beaufort Castle

"A fitful wind, Force 4 diminishing to Force 2, unsteadily blowing from West to South-East, Imminent"
bellowed the loud hailer at Beaufort Castle.

Moments after this Weather Warning, Wendy crash-landed straight into the middle of the Beaufort Courtyard early the next morning; her Wind-Force collapsed beneath her, completely blown out.

Indeed, the Earthling creature, flung onto the cloud-floor, was not only disheveled and pecked all over, but also completely winded.

'She's out cold,' announced Nanny Dover.

And, telling the children to stand back, bravely advanced to spray the body with Witch-hazel, followed by a strong sprinkling of her Lavender Talc, so they could all approach nearer.

'Dearest heart, what have they done to you?'

'Turned her Foul – that's what!' retorted Fisher. 'They've ruined her. Just look at the state of her!'

Plymouth tried ringing her Wind Chimes over the deplorable sight, then dared get nearer to take her temperature. It was exceedingly Low.

Dogger and Bailey came up with hot poultices to place on her wounds.

But Fastnet sensibly whizzed straight to the Cloud Computer and looked up: 'Foul to Fair. Help me! Help!'

The answer travelled through the atmosphere in an instant:

'Feed with Ambrosia creamed rice every day, and give a liberal dusting of lavender talc. Be gentle and encouraging.'

'Nanny is always right,' Fastnet thought, as she sped back.

Faeroes hung his head. He was the last to come to look at what had blown in. He tried invoking the Wind Gods for help – but to no avail.

Finisterre's Wind Force was put out to graze on the Beaufort lawn - and seemed relieved to be eating the Fairer cloud-fluff - while Nanny Dover was put in charge of keeping a Weather-eye on the Earthling.

'We have to give her time to recover. We must just wait.'

Later that day, Wendy suddenly sat up, terrified. She stared around at these new Weather-Creatures in astonishment, then began shaking with fear. There was a strong, distasteful lavender smell in the atmosphere. 'Where am I? Who are you all?'

'Don't be alarmed dear,' Said Nanny Dover, gently. 'You're at Beaufort Castle, and we're the Fair Weather-Makers. We need to help you to get Fair again like us, dear.'

But when Wendy saw these kindly creatures crowding round, and two young children – one with a Mermaiden's tail, she cried: 'Take me back to Heligoland. I need to be there – not here! I have to return to rescue Finisterre!'

The children called all the other Fair Weather-Makers to approach again, and Fisher, who was in charge of the Castle while Faeroes' energy was diminished, spoke to her gently.

'What do you mean, Earthling, explain,' he encouraged.

Wendy staggered to her feet, red in the face. She realized she'd have to tell them the truth. 'I resisted being cured so I could get back to save Finisterre - like she saved me. They've all gone soppy and in love. Finisterre did it to them with a spell in her wine during the Feast.'

'What Feast? Tell us.'

Once again, everyone drew nearer to listen. Faeroes was summoned from his bed.

'They've captured Finisterre. The Foul atmosphere will destroy her. She's already spoken Foul stuff herself during the fight. Don't you see, I have to stay Foul enough so I can get back there to help save her.'

Wendy burst into tears and began to shiver in such a scary way again, that Nanny grew alarmed. All her patient soothing would be undone. 'Don't alarm the child, so,' she glared. 'Hush, Wendy. Hush.'

But after her explanation, the Earthling swooned away once more, refusing to come round or respond to any entreaties.

Only Forties was brave enough to gather up the Foul little alien. Gently carrying the wasted creature, he posted her inside a soft cloud-duvet to lull her gently back to her senses, using some of the rhymes he used to quieten his agitated birds.

But Wizard Wight had stood some way away from the rest, stroking his beard, thinking hard. He'd noticed a heavy-looking backpack the Earthling carried, which had bounced sideways, and now lay unnoticed while the others administered to her.

Staring at it, the Wizard pierced it with his emerald eyes, and experienced a strong premonition. Quietly he lifted the bundle and disappeared with it up to his Turret. Wrenching open the backpack with trembling hands, he pulled out … the Tome … the cover of which, turned immediately to a bright purple beneath his touch.

'By the Sun's Own Splendor! Here, in my own hands, is my Brother, Wizard Cromarty's, magical book.

'But why would Finisterre send us this Tome if she's joined Heligoland? Surely, this Earthling must have been sent by Finisterre to help us? That must be it - surely.'

The Wizard caressed his find, turning pages, at first gingerly – then eagerly with ring-encrusted hands, while tears of joy tumbled from his cheeks to fizz … and strangely evaporate … on every page.

'Here, then, is a chance to restore our Castle to full working power … soon … maybe even make me Master of it - and this Foul Earthling has brought the Tome to us. I will keep this to myself for the moment.'

For several days, the Wizard was not seen. Locking his Turret door, he leaned greedily over the Tome's pages, poring over their wisdom, his beady eyes trying to comprehend the power emanating from every symbol. This new power he craved for himself - more than food, and he was filled with wonder as the volume lured him further and further inside itself, working with his brain for ways to use its Cabalistic signs.

But when he managed at last to group some of the most potent into an Equation, he realized that Beaufort, in its present lowered state, would not have nearly enough power for them to use it once formed. Sadly, Wizard Wight put the heavy Tome to one side, while he thought about what to do with it, and went down to join the others.

Fisher was in the process of holding a meeting.

'We really have to try turning the Earthling Fair before she expires. We're responsible now for her welfare and getting her back down to Earth.'

Fastnet agreed. 'Also, we need to extract more vital information from her about the state of Heligoland. And she might be able to inform us about the fate of poor Fair Isle's dangerous journey there beneath the seas.'

So Nanny Dover redoubled her efforts. She immersed the Earthling every morning in warm salty water, into which she tipped a tin of Epsom Salts and one of Andrew's Liver Salts as well … 'to cleanse the inner man' (as it said on the tin).

Nanny's gentleness seemed to work; though Wendy's eyes were still staring and wild, her face and arms bleached white with cold, her legs still a mass of cuts and bruises. But gradually she improved, looking Fairer every day. And when finally the Earthling grew warmer and came to her senses again, Nanny Dover clapped her hands to her chest, pleased her remedy had been successful.

The children called the other Fair Weather-Makers to approach again. Faeroes was informed, and at last left his bed.

Fastnet helped. She discovered an old dress that Fair Isle had knitted, patterned in bright Fair Isle colours, which was just right for Wendy; then, over the next few days, took it upon herself to encourage the Earthling to read 'Fair Ways with Weather' and learn how this was constructed.

Plymouth had a go with the Mermaiden's comb, attempting to untangle Wendy's mass of coppery-coloured hair, tousled into the worst knots she'd ever seen.

Faeroes despaired as he watched, remembering the way Fair Isle used it to comb out her own long locks. But the twins: Thames and Tyne, giggled at Wendy's screwed-up expressions when each knot was successfully untangled.

However, as she was recovering, Wendy began to wonder what had become of the Tome in her backpack. It must have been taken away from her after she'd crash-landed. But no-one had mentioned it. Why not?

She remembered the promise made to her Grandfather: his dying wish to search it out, then get it destroyed. She was strong enough now. It had to be somewhere in the castle hidden away from her.

The chance for Wendy to look around came when, with the joy of her recovery, Faeroes managed to get the Fair Weather-Makers to continue making a little secret War Weather again.

She explored everyone's quarters without success, until eventually, on reaching Wizard Wight's tall Turret and about to turn the door handle, she heard a voice from the interior muttering …

'But I need power … far more power to use them…'

Then, seeing Wendy at his open door, the Wizard called out - in a somewhat wheedling voice - 'Please, come in. Enter, Earthling, do.'

Wendy had not known that the Wizard made most of his weather-spells in his Turret. And here he was, actually consulting her Grandfather's Tome while, all around him, cloud coffers were propped open to show a myriad of sparkling spangles; and, over his head, cosmic orbs and heavenly spheres hung suspended from their cords, forming a tiny shining universe all of their own.

'As Guardian of Wizard Cromarty's Tome, tell me, Earthling Child, do you know how to power these symbols? I've entirely forgotten. Can you help me with them now you're recovered?'

He attempted to make his eyes glow with gentle encouragement. Here was help come at last.

But Wendy, seeing the Tome's cover changed to a fierce dark purple – and her own backpack flung forgotten in a corner - was reluctant to be friendly.

'No, sorry, I can't,' she replied. 'Only Grandfather knew.'

The Wizard's eyes dimmed. At first he looked crestfallen, then annoyed. This Earthling they'd spent so much time turning Fair, had turned out useless.

'Go away, then. Just go!'

Feeling ill-tempered, Wendy snatched up her backpack and left … and was about to run down the Wizard's cloud-cut stairs again … when she stopped.

There, cropping at the edge of the white Beaufort lawn below, fitter, and well filled-out … though away from the other Wind-Forces … was Finisterre's Backing Wind. She was probably not mixing well, as she was still partly Foul.

And an idea came: 'I'm fit enough now to blow away on her. I need to get back to Heligoland to rescue Finisterre. I'll do it tonight.'

But Wizard Wight wanted the Earthling out of the way. He'd grown sus-

113

picious of her actions, and wanted to keep the Tome for himself. During supper, he brazenly accosted her in front of them all.

'You've been creeping about the castle prying into things not your concern, Earthling, haven't you? Hasn't anyone wondered why it took so long turning her?'

'You mean you think she's been sent over here as some kind of spy?' Faeroes questioned, staring fixedly at Wendy.

'Yes, you heard her say that Finisterre had used Foul language.'

'Maybe you're right.' Fisher looked troubled. He frowned, causing some fog-tendrils to hover around his head. 'Maybe we should be keeping more of a weather-eye on her?'

'For the time being, then, Earthling girl,' Faeroes ordered, 'you're to stay in the Nursery, under Nanny's close supervision – until we know what's up in the atmosphere.'

And Wendy found her escape plan ruined.

Fisher frowned at the thought that the Earthling might be a spy, and for the first time, began doubting his beloved Finisterre's loyalty to Beaufort. 'Finisterre had good reason to change sides. But, listen – although we got her banned for creating Depressions ... we never heard her talk Foul.'

'However, if Finisterre did go there, couldn't she have managed to subdue the inhabitants in some way?' Plymouth suggested, hopefully. 'And that's why no weather's getting made by them.'

'That could be,' said Forties.

'Yes, perhaps that's why they haven't yet attacked? They would've been ready for War by now,' Faeroes looked relieved.

'Well I've been extracting more information from our birds', announced Forties. 'Something highly alarming is happening at Heligoland. A lot of my Sea-Birds squawk to say the Castle's gone quiet as Deep Down – and their Foul Feathered Force is quite out of hand.'

'Why didn't you tell me this straight away, Forties?' Faeroes looked annoyed; some emerald sparks shot from his eyes.

'I thought it only chitchat … the way birds do go on …'

'Anything more?' His nerves were almost frayed to splitting point.

'Only that our Fair Weather-Birds'll no longer go anywhere near the place.

114

They're afeared. But one Guillemot from Maplin Sands told me that the White Witch would never go over to Heligoland.'

'Faeroes frowned. 'It does sound like the Foul Weather-Makers have lost power and it's only the Foul Weather-Birds birds in control.'

'Shouldn't we try to attack them first, then?' Fastnet suggested.

'No!' Wizard Wight stood and swirled his clock to be impressive. 'We haven't enough power. We need to make ourselves much, much stronger. We're not nearly ready. What has happened to everyone? What's happening to Beaufort?'

'It's the Earthling girl's state - and you, King Faeroes, being infected that's put us in such a Low condition,' Nanny scolded. 'With your sadness at Fair Isle's disappearance, and Finisterre maybe becoming Foul is what's getting all of us down. The atmosphere of the Castle's been upset. No-one's any energy left to prepare properly for War. Everyone's listless.'

Their Leader hung his head. It was true - all his power had drifted away. Leaving the others, Faeroes went sadly back to his room, where he fell onto his featherbed and wept once more, heaving with silent steady rain.

At this relapse in their Leader, soon, no weather of any kind was being made, and Wendy was prevented from leaving Nanny's Nursery.

They were just living off their supplies of tinned sardines.

Before long, the whole castle had succumbed to a considerable bout of Anticyclonic Gloom.

During the rest of February, there was no weather at all over the British Isles. Neither Beaufort nor Heligoland were making any.

Even the air itself grew still.

Throughout the British Isles, the people, too, felt at first uneasy, then scared. Many boarded up their homes and took in supplies.

And when the situation continued, the British lost their remaining faith in Mr Allbright, the Weatherman (who now suspected that his public realized he'd only been guessing every day when he predicted the weather.)

'It's all so confusing,' he thought. 'It's as if ... as if the weather was controlled by a curious energy in the air itself ... a strange force somewhere high in the path of the clouds floating over Britain and over the seas ... in a place where the weather is thinner, the oxygen rarer, and only sea-birds can breathe.'

He began to worry about the Chaos Theory: how the simple wave of a butterfly's wing in one part of the world could alter weather conditions at the other end of the globe … it was all so mysterious …

But the more he thought about things, the more he became worried whether it was perhaps their own behaviour down on earth causing this conflict in the skies. For example:

Why were the prevailing winds behaving strangely?

Why had the Jet Stream wavered?

Why were ocean currents becoming altered …?

Questions, too, had been raised in the House of Commons over the disappearance of the girl from the roof of the Weather Station. Murmurings became more persistent.

Accusations were made by Wendy's mother, quite beside herself with worry; also Wendy's school-friends and relations kept nagging the Press for information.

So a Public Enquiry was held and, in the embarrassment that followed, the main Meteorological Office in Exeter was forced to shut down.

With no Weather Reports, the British grew really alarmed. Widespread insecurity settled on all parts of the country.

With no Shipping Forecasts, ships would not set out.

With no proper wind to lift their wings into the sky, airplanes were loath to take off.

Without any weather the hosts of dinner parties were at a loss: there was absolutely nothing whatsoever to talk about.

In the period of economic instability that followed, the Stock Market fell, and the currency devalued. With a General Election forthcoming, the United Kingdom, once powerful and prestigious, was brought to its knees.

At Beaufort Castle, King Faeroes turned over and over in his sleep on his soft white foam-bed, searching the empty space beside him for his Mermaid Wife. 'Fair Isle, where are you? Swim back to me,' he called.

And from her dreams, Wendy pleaded for Finisterre: 'I want to be with you forever. Let me go back to rescue you.'

At the White Witch's Sunny Intervals Residence, Stormy Petrels and Razorbills had landed in the windless skies, daring to roost like a layer of dust on Finisterre's lovely white cloud-lawn.

In Heligoland Hall, the stagnant air was occasionally filled with weird dream-weather, made by those in their troubled sleep.

A dismal fog from Malin's mind sagged and folded against the rampart walls; some low leaden clouds from Sole's imagination shifted around, bumping one into another to produce occasional sleet …

And sometimes Biscay would rise above her nervous breakdown to feel her way along to the Heligoland Wind-organ to play a dreadful dirge.

Down in the dungeon, Finisterre's face twitched. A black power, creeping slowly, covered her mind as she slipped down towards death.

But deeper inside her, Fitzroy smiled crookedly in his sleep. 'It's coming,' he sighed. 'My black evil is on its way,' My darkness will soon be here.'

Under the cover of darkness, a Mermaiden swam along the south coast of Britain using, as her guide, all the Light Houses and Light Ships along the coast. Luckily, the waves were pretty flat with only the current and no wind to push them along.

By interpreting the lengths of their flashes, Fair Isle could tell exactly where she was, and, without any ships setting sail, she had the feeling they were winking just for her.

And when no friendly lights were visible, Fair Isle rolled over on her back to read the stars, which were totally unobscured by clouds.

She only dared travel at night, resting by day amongst long strands of kelp for camouflage – though nothing seemed to be flying in the skies.

She ate such food as Mermaidens do from the sea.

Part 5

Chapter 18
Black Magic.

Hebrides the Black Witch streaked like one of the Furies through the emptied skies back to Heligoland Hall. Her convalescence in Foulness had been a success; her wand was now completely recharged. Filled with a new urgent power, she would exact her revenge on the White Witch for the love-spell she had put on the Foul Weather-Makers.

But when she landed, she saw only a pathetic wind worrying aimlessly at their sullen Wind-sock, which hung limply and had acquired yet another hole in its heel since she last saw it.

An uncontrolled drizzle drifted in forgotten banks across the Turrets; a restless sea surged sluggishly against the ramparts. The whole place had sunk so low over the Irish Sea that it barely floated above the waves.

'Out of my way!' Hebrides shrieked, now choking with rage as she threw open the front door.

Starved Sea-Rats rushed out to greet her, followed by Warty Toads hopping, and Sea–Serpents slithering.

Everywhere, Hebrides was met by an atmosphere of despondency, lethargy and defeat 'I needed to do this to all you Weather-Makers. It was to save you from the White Witch's power,' she muttered.

She found Malin, lying stiff as a board outside the Master Bedroom, with chilblains on both hands and feet.

She looked in on Sole who, with red swollen eyes, lay on her bed, rocking gently on a sea of salty tears. Her body was propped against a mountain of pillows stuffed in every crevice with paper hankies, looking more like a Cormorant's nesting-place.

'Black! Black!' Hebrides screamed. 'Give me something dark and evil to destroy this curse.' Her hands tightened round her robes as high-heeled boots kicked open her Turret door, and slammed it shut. There was serious business she had to attend to right away.

Taking a piece of chalk in her fingers – (a sharpened sliver she'd hacked from the end of the Needles as she hurried by), Hebrides described a large arc around herself on the floor.

Now she was ready to construct a strong security wall for her magic.

First, she pulled in her iron cauldron (which she used occasionally to brew up a storm), then grabbed some theatrical props, and hung these with blackout curtains for a screen. The remaining gaps were filled with Weather-charts, spell-books and some dead men's bones.

Into the completed circle she stepped with her orb.

With her wand dancing through the air, Dark Energy was already collecting around her. Electricity hummed, earthing in a hurry, first through the cauldron, then fizzing into her iron bedstead.

Next, the Black Witch polished the surface of the crystal with her velvet petticoat and, spreading bony hands over the orb, grasped it until her knuckles bleached white.

Stolen gold rings from her wrecks glinted on her fingers as the power level rose.

Beyond the magic circle, Warty Toads croaked, Sea-Serpents hissed, the eyes of Sea-Rats glowed conspiratorially.

Hebrides' own eyes rolled inwards, then up into their lids.

Soon she'd left her body altogether and, whirling upwards, condensed into a tiny knot. She worked using mostly negative forces: black neutrons, electro-magnetic waves, anti-matter, quarks.

As she concentrated, her crystal crackled, then spat out noises, like air escaping from a drowned man's lungs.

Suddenly, the orb turned jet black; its surfaces filmed over with a delicate webbing of a sticky substance. Coming back into her body, Hebrides rolled down her eyes and smiled sweetly at her creatures.

'My crystal has promised me IMMINENT DOOM.'

Then, exhausted, she climbed into her bed.

During the small hours of the morning, Fitzroy's oil-slick oozed its way quietly towards Heligoland.

Unhampered by any weather, it was able to flow along, first by inertia, then helped along on a sluggish sea-current that favoured its direction.

Finding the Foul Castle as an obstacle in its path, it began to divide. The central part of the slick stopped, but the edges moved gently onwards.

The two outer arms felt their way carefully around the ramparts and touched again on the further side. There they remained clasped, holding Heligoland in a strong embrace.

The Mermaiden, Fair Isle, swam right up to the Irish Sea at last, aiming for Latitudes 52 and 55 degrees North, Longitudes 5 and 7 South, towards Heligoland.

After a while, she came to a sudden halt. Though dawn had broken, everything had become strangely dark overhead. There was no way up. Frightened, Fair Isle turned tail, reversed her strokes sharply, until the edge of the darkness was just above. Only then did she dare to surface.

And there, right in front of her, in the first weak rays of dawn, barely floating in the centre of an enormous black lawn of tar, she saw what must be Heligoland Hall.

She shuddered at its appearance: it seemed to be imprisoned like some giant squid, with its gluey black ink spilled out in a sea-skirt all around itself.

Fair Isle touched the spongy edge of the slick. A collection of flotsam and jetsam was stuck to it: polythene bags, buckets, toothbrushes, a child's pink plastic school backpack, a large polythene barrel with one end bashed out – all the usual cast-offs from the Earthlings' unthinking way of life.

She tried to climb the plastic to get onto the slick, but it was so slippery it needed several attempts. By the time she'd managed it, her fishy body was smeared dark as the tar itself, and her lovely long seaweedy hair transformed into a mop of pitch-coloured serpentine wriggles. Thus disguised, she bravely slithered forth.

The Foul Feathered Force, wheeling aimlessly above, looked down at the squirming creature. They thought about attacking it … but it looked as Foul as they were, so they ignored it.

By the time the Mermaiden slid easily right to the ramparts, she felt mysteriously rejuvenated after her long-distance swimming, and was filled with a curious buzz of energy. She was pleased to have gone instead of Fisher to rescue the girl; and Faeroes would never have made it. Now she felt strong enough to be able to rescue the Earthling girl and support her all the way back to Beaufort.

She saw no sign of activity around the castle until, reaching a prison grille, she managed to raise herself up on to the end of her fishy tail and, balancing carefully, peered through the bars.

As her eyes accustomed themselves to the dim light within, she noticed the inert body of Finisterre. 'By Borealis! Is our Finisterre sleeping or dead? Have I done this all for nothing?'

She was about to call to her through the grille, when she heard the metallic rattling of something being dragged along the ramparts above. It was obviously far too dangerous to try to raise her voice to Finisterre's inert body inside during daylight hours; somebody was definitely around. Better to try later, beneath the protection of dusk.

Remembering the plastic barrel, Fair Isle slithered back to the edge of the slick and rested inside, curled around its inner shape to sleep.

'Only one thing might have saved Finisterre from freezing to death,' she thought as she drifted off: 'Finisterre was wearing her special seaweed shawl, which shrank when she was warm and swelled up around her when she was cold. That might just be enough to have saved her – Also, there's no Foul weather around Heligoland to have frozen her to death.'

The metallic rattling Fair Isle heard, had been made by Lundy dragging her largest pan along the Ramparts.

Earlier on, the Cook's nose had twitched at the pleasant oily smell filtering down into where she'd fallen in love with Viking deep inside her mammoth sugar bin after the Dance. This had filled the vacuum where her lover had been, infusing the space with a pleasing acrid odour.

Roused by this, the Cook climbed out, shook herself free of the sugar … only to find her Kitchen oppressively dark. The fire had gone out long ago. Little light penetrated the window.

'Somethin's diffrent!' she declared. She hauled her largest pan over to the window and stood on it to survey the scene properly outside.

For several minutes she watched the oil slick, which covered where the sea had once been, and considered its possibilities. Then, full of excitement, she dragged the pan outside, rumbling it roughly over the ramparts towards the black stuff.

The blackness strangely excited her; it was as if it had awoken her and brought her out of a long, dark sleep.

'Pollution is the Solution,' she decided, using her ladle to trawl up some mussels from the deep, which, on their way up, were drenched automatically in a rich, oily sauce.

Hebrides awoke at last, having recovered from her last night's ordeal. Sitting bolt upright, knowing they were in the grip of something very important, she sprang ecstatically from her bed.

'The Doom my crystal promised me has arrived!' she cried.

For several minutes she leaned from her window, gloating.

Blackness covered the ocean much as it had covered her crystal orb.

She dashed downstairs, to where Lundy's Moules Tar-tar were being prepared for breakfast.

With one bolt of forked lightning Hebrides lit a newly-stacked fire beneath them. Soon, a bitter grey smoke arose from the largest pan.

As the sauce began to bubble, both Hebrides and Lundy tried some. The thick embroilment was vicious, burning their lips, leaving their tongues as furred up as an old sealskin coat; then it seared its way down into their stomachs.

'P.e.r.f.e.c.t' Hebrides rasped, clutching her throat. 'Th.i.s. sh.ould. do the Tri.ck! How I shall make them suffer!'

While Lundy laid the table for an oily breakfast, she discovered that their Captain Humber had fallen under the Dining-room table after the feast, and had passed into his second childhood. He looked tattered and rather smaller.

'*One staccato on the Needles*
Boomer two and three,
Four short blasts on the great Bell Rock
And one long, loud Tireeee,'
the rattling man sang reedily when he saw her.

Lifting him carefully, Lundy carried their chalky-brained Leader to the Master Bedroom. His body, covered in phantom barnacles and other creeping things, weighed practically nothing and was almost completely dissolved into thin air.

Stepping over the recumbent Malin, who had fallen asleep outside this room he loved, she posted Humber into his ice-cold bed. 'He'll not be needing any tar – our ancient Leader's end is nigh,' she sighed.

Indeed, Humber was already dreaming of joining his wife, Shannon, imagining that her pale crystalline body was lying on the lumpy stratified cloud-covering beside him, her frigid hand locked tightly into his. She was giving him kisses as hard as the frost of which she'd been in charge. (But this was really Lundy kissing him goodbye).

'Winter is a strange device
For turning water into ice'

were the final words he mumbled to her.

Lundy thought this needed some sort of reply, but the best that she could come up with, as she closed his eyelids, was:

'And Summer is a pleasant whim
For taking off the clothes to swim.'

Humber seemed quite happy with it, however.

He smiled as his eyes fogged over and he expired.

A coil of smoky tar leaking through the aperture in her chimney next morning awoke the dry-eyed Sole. It was an aroma more soothing to her sore throat than any cough mixture. Diving off her bed, she swam through her tears to the window where, by treading water, she was able to pull aside seaweed curtains to force her rusty window ajar.

She saw oil stretching in a vast layer; its edges rounded off like a currant bun. It lapped to and fro intriguingly, making a pleasant slurping sound against their castle walls, leaving long streaks of brown … 'almost like little hands reaching up, losing grip, then sliding down again,' she thought, smiling; pleased it had come to stay.

Viking arose with a snort, ran swiftly to the ramparts and, finding the hole Lundy had made when gathering mussels, plunged in. After a short swim and a complete covering of slick, he arose brown, dripping and oiled … then gave himself a thorough beating with a plank.

Lundy's mind, which had been sharpened by the oil, suddenly reminded her that something very important to her was missing.

She wasn't afraid of Hebrides so, approaching the Black Witch, threatened her with her ladle. 'By the way, Hebrides, where's my little Helper, Windy? Why won't you tell me where she's gone? What have you done with her?'

'Never you mind, Lundy; where's German Bight?' Hebrides retorted. 'Why hasn't he appeared for Breakfast? I asked you to take him down some oil while I laid out our Captain's ghost in the Hall.'

'I did. He's still in the Study where you left him – and he doesn't want none.'

'We'll soon see about that!' Hebrides grabbed a large bowl of Moules Tar-tar, and marched towards his Study.

She found the Toad Paperweight greedily slurping from the bowl Lundy had left earlier. As it gulped, its eyes bulged with enormous venom. Its size at first doubled, then tripled. Hebrides kicked the monstrous creature aside, then forced the remains of Toad's bowl of tar down GB's throat.

Instantly, his body began to writhe. He sat bolt upright, his hair standing on end, the monocle clenched fiercely in his left eye ... then: 'Finisterre,' he moaned, sinking back into a state of melancholy.

Hebrides frowned. 'Why aren't you being cured like the rest?'

Then she saw lying beside him, the magazine '*Weather or Not*'.

'Curses, I'd forgotten about the spell the White Witch put on that photograph of herself !'

Hebrides sat down and, putting her head between her hands, wept as if she were Sole. She realized that her original feelings towards GB, those of pos-sessiveness and jealousy, still remained. She needed him badly: they still had to create a War Equation – but now they had no Tome to work from. And she was particularly worried that Malin would be made the new Leader instead of him.

Suddenly, she was deeply worried about what she'd done to her rival. 'That White Witch still has a hold over him with that curse on the 'Weather or Not' cover ... and I left her to rot. Not only did I allow Windy to escape with our precious Tome, but I sent Finisterre to her doom precisely when I needed to bargain with her. If she's expired, then GB will never be saved. Malin will become Leader.'

Hebrides heard Viking blow the Foghorn urgently for breakfast, but what she needed to check first was far more important. Grabbing the dungeon key from where it hung by GB's door, she put it in her pocket.   Then, lifting her skirts with one hand, she balanced the second bowl of tar sauce in the other and raced along to the dungeon to unlock it.

She was too late – the White Witch's body lay slumped on the ground. Next to it, a confusion of empty limpet-shells lay scattered across the dungeon floor. Looking at these more closely, however, Hebrides realized that they formed German Bight's Cabalistic Equation.

'So, she must've spotted it written on GB's blackboard, and was in the process of completing it.'

Her eyes swept across the Equation like a lighthouse lamp searching for ships to save. 'She would've kept herself alive on these crustaceans, but seems to have collapsed before she could eat the final part ... and that last part has managed to crawl away ... the part, unfortunately, we need. However, if the first part of the Equation was keeping her going, there's hope yet she's still alive ...'

She wrenched open Finisterre's mouth and forced the complete contents of the bowl down.

'I've suffered your magic, White Witch; now you can try some of mine. I need you alive.'

Fitzroy, who'd taken over, caught its burning firewater first. He choked, burped loudly – and wow! That slick he'd directed towards Heligoland had real kick to it. 'You mean MY magic, Black Witch!' he thought. Then Finisterre spluttered and also came to. First, her eyes sprang open, then, as the fiery stuff raced downwards, her muscles oozed with unnatural oily strength.

Drawing her newly-charged wand from the top of her boot, Hebrides said 'White Witch, I can demolish you with one stroke of this wand ... but I'll save your life if you restore German Bight to me.'

'Haven't you already managed to restore him with some of this oily stuff? It's certainly restored us ... I mean, me.' Finisterre found she could flex her arms and legs. She felt unbelievably full of zest.

'Yes, oil produces huge energy, as you well know. But German Bight is only half-well. You've bewitched him in some other way.'

Finisterre looked puzzled, then remembered: 'Oh yes, my magazine 'Weather or Not', wasn't it, Black Witch? Well, my answer is, you mustn't only save my life,' she replied, calmly, 'you have to let me go ... allow me to escape from here.'

'Never!' The Black Witch stamped. 'That would be too much! The others would evaporate me!' She stormed off, and was in the process of slamming the dungeon door shut when …

'I can finish solving the rest of the Equation for you!' shouted the Fitzroy part of the White Witch. 'Easily! I can complete it from what you wrote on German Bight's blackboard in his Study. My father, Wizard Cromarty, taught me all about the Cabalistic signs when I was young.'

The Black Witch frowned. Wizard Cromarty was her father as well; so that made the White Witch her sister! A sister who their mother, Gaia Celeste, discovering she was Fair, not Foul, must have taken to Beaufort to be brought up, while she, Hebrides, stayed behind at Heligoland Hall.

The Black Witch suddenly felt herself softening towards her Fair sister; and - recalling this sister's more attractive Foul voice from their fight – she realized that this must mean there was some of Wizard Cromarty's Foulness inside Finisterre. 'I agree, then to help you escape,' she said; 'but it'll have to be done secretly.'

… She was also hurriedly working out something else important: just supposing she were to present the others with the completed Equation by tomorrow at Breakfast, ready for them to use to wage War … but as if solved by German Bight … then that would make him eligible to claim his rightful position as their new Leader instead of Malin.

'It'll be difficult to get you away,' she said, returning to what they were saying.

'Then why don't you simply say "the White Witch and her wand have lost all their power - so I didn't bother to restore her with any oil as she's practically expired,' Finisterre suggested, back in her own voice. 'That'll make things easier, surely.'

'A clever solution, White Witch … however … how do I know that the Equation you give me will be correct?'

'You won't – but German Bight certainly will when he sees it.'

'He cannot – unless you restore him to me by tomorrow morning.'

'And I cannot do that until I return to Sunny Intervals tonight. And you'll have to return my wand in order to recharge it to undo the spell. So we'll just have to trust one another, won't we?'

128

'Witch's Word?'

'Witch's Word.'

They both spat on the floor like the Sister Witches they were, and the bargain was sealed.

Chapter 19
Sea-Slugs Gloriosa

H ebrides entered the Dining Hall just as Breakfast was over.
     She found Malin standing on his chair announcing to them all …

'Now that our dear Captain Humber is no longer with us … and with neither German Bight nor Hebrides bothering to appear… I'm pleased to appoint myself your new Leader.'

Grinding one black boot hard into the ground, Hebrides turned on him.

'No, Malin, I've decided I will be Leader of Heligoland Hall.'

'Y… you …' Malin stuttered … 'But you're a woman!'

'I'm well aware of that, Malin. I assure you I'm quite capable of leading you. I restored you all, so I'm allowed to be in charge.'

The idea of being Leader had come to Hebrides in a lighthouse-flash, and her eyes were beaming as brightly as a lighthouse-lamp.

'You have to admit, everyone, that after devouring the *Moules Tar-tar* which Lundy and I prepared for Breakfast, every one of you Weather-Makers is not only fully recovered, but filled with unimaginable strength … and the reason German Bight's not here, is … is … that he's working non-stop to resolve the Equation for us. It'll be ready, he assures us, by this time tomorrow.

Oh, and by the way, Finisterre, the White Witch, won't be causing us any more problems. She's safely in the dungeon overcome by me and practically expired. And I took away her wand, which has lost all its power after our fight – so I didn't bother to restore her with any oil.'

Then, needing to assert her authority, she brought them to attention by saying,

'Haven't you all forgotten something? There's a War on!

So now, with your strength completely restored by the tar, I want everyone out testing the slick for its possibilities … but still doing this secretly, behind my curtain of mist. Go out and get started.'

Malin scowled. Before he went outside, he decided to disobey their new Lady Leader by having one last look at his rightful Master Bedroom …
'It'll belong to her now,' he spat.

Opening the door a crack to view the thing he'd fallen in love with at the Feast, he stared inside longingly. Now the Master bedroom was lost to him forever.

His eyes alighted on Humber's wind-up plastic duck. 'I'll just take that then.'

Grabbing it from the bedside table, he went out to where the slick slurped at the castle's edge. Winding the duck fully, he sent it whirring furiously over the flat surface to test its possibilities. To his delight, it scudded into the distance at great speed without being stuck. Malin was satisfied. After oiling his knees, he could follow with ease – and the stuff did absolute wonders for his arthritis.

Hebrides continued proving her dominance during the rest of the day: 'Get a cold grip on yourself!' she admonished Viking; 'Pull up your socks!' she ordered Sole, who was drizzling tentatively towards the frightening black surface.

Bravely then, the dismal creature ventured out to practice a little rain. At first she was baffled: her tears refused to sink, forming, instead, small puddles and inland seas; but soon she was causing a downfall, which cascaded prettily over the slick's edge.

Viking disappeared into his forge to oil his Thundering Equipment.

Biscay, being a practical lady, first waterproofed her mac with a coating of tar to protect her from Sole's rain, and then courageously took two of her smallest Wind-Forces out for an airing on the slick. They blew superbly over its polished surface as if it were an ice-sheet.

Only Lundy grumbled. She'd been ordered to cook Wartime Food.

'How can I cope without my Little Helper what's been blown away? I want her back. Nobody tells me where she's gone.'

Lundy sulked, having to pick sea-slugs off the shredded sea-cabbage herself. She needed to mix them with some of the tar to get Windy's particular shade of grey-green mayonnaise that everyone liked.

Grudgingly, she later made a stab in a Wartime direction by stamping her food 'Warning: high tar content'.

But something very strange was happening.

Once they'd devoured her oil-soaked Sea-slugs Gloriosa, the Foul

Weather-Makers were invigorated further and further after every mouthful.

Hebrides contemplated with amazement the 'Doom' the orb had promised - this black blanket of unrefined oil had brought them all untold energy. 'My orb was correct; "Pollution IS the Solution,"' she stated. 'Now, at last, we can continue with our War.'

At Supper she was strong enough to announce:

'My plan - once GB completes his Cabalistic Equation tomorrow morning - is not only to defeat the Fair Weather-Makers and blow Beaufort Castle apart – which will be easy now without the White Witch to help them. Then I intend, with all your help, to subdue the British Isles … after that, maybe even the whole of Europe … then, possibly … what about the whole planet?'

Her eyes shot out rays of pleasure … 'Think of it … we could alter the whole wide world's weather-patterns with our pollution! But in order for this plan to succeed, it's essential for us all to work hard, and still make it secretly behind our their curtain of grey mist.

… And that includes you, Malin … if you want to be part of it. Do you?'

Malin stiffened, freezing up the blood around his heart.

Hebrides had already showered upon him all the extra work Humber used to do: carving snowflakes, manufacturing his dead wife's frost ...

But Hebrides was a smarter operator: yes, it would be GB she'd choose for her Second … but she was also aware that to win a Weather War, Malin's full support would be vital. So she added:

'By the way, Malin, I've decided you can have the Master Bedroom.

I, myself, have no use for it. I'm quite satisfied with my own sweet Turret.'

At this news, Malin underwent a complete body-change.

His heart unfroze, allowing him to bow to his new Leader, before striding straight up to the beloved room.

There, he caressed the four-poster, crushed in his fists its lumpy Fulmer-feathered mattress, ran his hand over the cold linen sheets. Finally, flinging open the windows, he let some stray drizzle in to dampen down the covers.

In Lundy's Kitchen, even the Foul Weather-Birds were being fortified.

By pressing their beaks sideways against the Kitchen window and seeing Lundy cook once more, they clamoured for some strengthening food.

Lundy obliged them for a change, and kindly threw them pieces carved off her slab of Crude Liquorice Allsorts, which maddened them considerably and made them scream fiercely …

… but at the same time, she laid one or two down in a sea-salt barrel for her new War Effort. 'After all, once they're tarred and feathered, who's to know whether they be Fair nor Foul?'

Biscay was pleased the new Leader was a woman like herself. Knotting her headscarf resolutely beneath her chin, and aware she was cutting a trim figure in a new pair of jodhpurs and gumboots, she postured with a blustery look in her eyes and a new seaweed whip in her hands. Confidently then, she took a whole team of Wind-Forces out onto the slick. Even the weakest sped over its surface under her control, and it wasn't long before she'd trained them up to Force 7, even Force 8.

'I'm ready now to reform an exceedingly wild 'Foul Feathered Force,' she declared … 'then maybe she'll choose me as her Second-In-Command.'

All day long, Sole rained so hard into some huge new Header Tanks Viking had constructed in his forge, that they were soon overflowing.

He himself produced so many admirable thunderbolts to store, that he needed to plunge from the battlements into Lundy's tar-hole to cool himself down.

Their new Leader, Hebrides, worked on several complicated positive and negative charges to make them crackle as lightning-strokes inside the Storm Clouds.

Malin, meanwhile, turned out rack after rack of thick gray, stratified clouds, which showed in their neatly-stacked piles, an uninspired sameness.

And, as he churned each layer in endless repetition, he almost felt what it was like to be happy.

133

Chapter 20
KR Magnetic 2

Just as dusk was falling and a gibbous moon glinted dimly over the tarry surface, Fair Isle wriggled out of her barrel. She'd been worried by noises magnified from its interior during the day: howling winds, ringing crashes, and most bizarrely … and perhaps most frightening of all … something sounding just like a mechanical toy, quacking as it tracked along.

But now she found she had to penetrate a strange wall of greyness, swirling in a thick disguising sheet between her and the prison grille. So, using instinct alone, she slid through it without difficulty.

She passed a window where clapping and merriment issued forth, and realized that the inhabitants were all at their evening meal.

Reaching the dungeon again, she raised herself on her tail to sing softly a verse of 'Sweet and High', projecting it through the grille.

The effect was immediate. 'Fair Isle! Is that really you?'

The White Witch made her way over, using a lot of effort to keep Fitzroy deep down inside her. 'Goodness! You look quite extraordinary under that dark disguise,'

'You're alive, Finisterre! How wonderful! No, this isn't a disguise; it's all this black tar. It's taken me ages to swim all this way, but now I've got here, I find this oily stuff has restored my energy.'

'Yes, I feel great as well with it – full of renewed strength,'

'But where's the Earthling, Finisterre? I came to rescue both of you.'

'I was able to send her away on my Backing Wind to safety … But I have to tell you that Wendy turned Foul during her stay here at Heligoland … and she must be turned Fair again, before being sent safely back to Earth'.

'And another thing, Fair Isle: Wendy took Wizard Cromarty's Tome away with her to Beaufort, and this has to be destroyed as soon as possible when you get back. Heaven knows what that evil Tome will do in Beaufort - if Wizard Wight gets hold of it.'

'Yes, we'll do what we can at Beaufort; but, more immediately, how am I going to rescue you?' said Fair Isle, thinking that Finisterre was looking wretchedly thin and alarmingly wild-eyed; altogether rather alien; in fact, more than a little untrustworthy…

'You don't have to worry about me, Fair Isle. We … I mean … I'm going to be sent back home … in exchange for giving them the completed Cabalistic Equation. It's over there! I managed to work it out using some empty limpet-shells. We've – I've just completed it in return for Hebrides releasing me tonight.'

'Oh, Finisterre! You've deceived us! As soon as Heligoland forges **War Weather** using this Equation, Beaufort's doomed. We thought you were still on our side …'

'It's amazing I am … seeing you banished me as you all did.'

Finisterre sighed. She knew she would have to help Beaufort, as both Fisher and the Earthling child were there. But even if Wizard Wight was able to form an Equation from the Tome, she knew in her heart that Beaufort simply wasn't strong enough any more to be able to use it to wage a War. …but then suddenly she thought of a brilliant way she could help them.

'Listen, Fair Isle, could you memorize this Equation then swim with it back to Beaufort? Then they'd at least be able to use the finished Equation to counteract what Heligoland is doing. I'm afraid I can't do anything just yet; when I get home to Sunny Intervals, I'll need some time to recover before I can help anyone with anything.'

'Oh No! Finisterre, I can't remember Equations - you know I can't. Mermaids just cannot do mathematics – every thing I do works only with the rhythm of the seas. The moment I try putting figures into my head, they start to creep away. This tarry stuff has strengthened my body - not sharpened my mind.' Fair Isle was beginning to lose her balance.

'Try, Fair Isle. You've got to. It'll mean certain defeat for you all at Beaufort unless you do.'

But the more Fair Isle tried, the more she was unable to get the Equation in the right order in her head. 'Everything turns into a kind of white water. I can't. Really I can't. I'd remember it all wrong. Mermaids really do not need mathematics inside the sea,' she wailed, as salty tears ran tar-channels down each cheek.

'If I had my wand here, I might be able to help you; you won't know this, but – after I was banished – I went to see Portland Bill who strengthened me with his special Light Therapy and made my wand and orb much more powerful.

But my orb's back at Sunny Intervals, and the Black Witch has stolen my wand – which had run out of power anyway - so I'm unable to use a single one of my spells to help you, Fair Isle.'

'Stop right there, Finisterre!' Fair Isle cried. 'I've just thought of something. There is another way we could try: we could use your orb for ESP; if we use the same frequencies. Come really close to me, so I can check.'

'Sshh! Someone will hear you - in fact I can hear someone.'

'Quick then! Come Closer!'

Fair Isle looked deeply into Finisterre's eyes. 'Yes! You do now have the capability of using Extra Sensory Perception. Listen! You could relay the Equation to me, Finisterre, when you return to Sunny Intervals, and then, once I reach Beaufort, I'll stay receptive. I used KR Magnetic 2 under the sea, and I'm good at using that frequency. See if you can match that and …'

But now the dungeon door was opening; the Black Witch striding in, holding paper and one of GB's green biros ready in her hands. She failed to catch a glimpse of a black Mermaid flipping down from the grille, but stared straight down at the Equation – and knew it to be correct.

'Congratulations, White Witch! Write it down. Hurry!'

No longer would the Black Witch need to worry that the Earthling had absconded with the Tome. Its important Equation to win a **Weather War now was almost hers.**

During dessert that evening, the Black Witch cleverly opened bottles of her best and strongest green plankton wine ready for the others to drink … to keep them occupied. She told them she was taking a glass down to German Bight to help him complete the final piece of Equation - and so was able to slip away from the Dining Hall.

Hebrides, however, got up to something altogether different:

She constructed a special piece of weather, harnessing her full, new, oily power to get the White Witch safely from the castle: a sheet of thick Fog. And it was not bad as Fogs go; it billowed nicely yellow and opaque; it whirled around itself, squashed down hard on the tar, borrowing brownness from the oil to ease its flow. Quickly, the Black Witch flattened this out and wound it up ready for Finisterre's escape.

Then she fetched the White Witch from the dungeon.

'Come with me - Now! And quietly! I've prepared that second Fair Wind-Force for you to ride – the one you had to carry the crates of wine here for the Feast - It's waiting impatiently for you. And I've manufactured a clever piece of weather, inside which you can escape.'

With that, she ushered Finisterre onto the Heligoland battlements, where her second Wind-Force was prancing in a barely controllable manner under the stars. Hebrides had force-fed it rather a lot of Sea-cucumber... coated in tar.

Next, Hebrides deftly unrolled her Fog sheet and began altering it into something far more powerful.

Carefully and expertly, she twisted the Fog as tight as it would go, condensing its material into a long woven tube, stronger than a sailor's rope. Then the prisoner found herself - after several attempts - mounting her unsteady steed.

'Here, White Witch, you'll need your wand back again to recharge in order to release the spell on German Bight when you reach your Residence. I discovered I was unable to use it myself – it only answers to you ... In you go!' Hebrides hissed, roughly pushing Finisterre inside the Fog Funnel...'and be quite sure to keep your side of the bargain: undo that curse on *Weather or Not!'*

The Fog Funnel sucked the White Witch up inside its Foul yellow smog and, by gaining immense speed from the slick's lubrication, by drawing oily air into itself like fuel, it lifted off its runway, spinning away faster and faster into the air, hiding its rider entirely from view.

Inside it, Finisterre/Fitzroy found themselves buffeted from one side of the inner spinning vortex to the other, as they clung to their Wind-Force for dear life.

But what Hebrides failed, to notice, was:
a black Mermaiden, flipping and sliding to the end of the slick.

There, where dim starlight and the gibbous moon lit up the child's backpack, still stuck to its edge, she grabbed one of the plastic bags stuck to the end of the slick, and quickly scooped black oily slick-substance to fill it full. Then putting this inside the backpack, she wiped more tar over the backpack's pink exterior to make it invisible.

It fitted perfectly when she strapped it onto her back, and was easy to carry using her new tarry strength.

And then, like the slimiest of eels, she did a strong crawl away from

Heligoland Hall.

 And what Hebrides also failed to notice as she headed indoors, was:

That, at the precise moment when Finisterre was blown into her Fog Funnel,

a strong Backdraft whipped the seaweed shawl off her shoulders,

whisked it high into the air,

twisted it into a reverse spin like exhaust from a rocket,

sent it over the Heligoland chimney-pots into the calm centre of the Low,

where it stalled,

lost momentum,

and slithered down one of the chimneys, right into the Dining Hall

… just as its occupants were raising a toast to their new Leader.

 Malin recognized instantly the White Witch's shawl descending like a crinkled sea-snake into the fireplace. There, it sizzled and spat at them.

 'Hebrides, you said the White Witch hadn't been given any oil and had almost evaporated – but she hasn't at all, has she! She's escaping, isn't she?' he yelled. 'Who let your prisoner go? It has to be German Bight.'

 'No, he's in his dungeon drinking the wine I just took down to him, and he's hard at work finishing the Equation. It must be you, Sole – or Lundy…?

 'It wasn't me,' Sole burst into hurtful tears.

 'And I never!' heaved Lundy, indignantly.

 'Then, Viking, throw out your strongest storm! Biscay, follow that with your wildest winds! I want her dead by the morning,' ordered Hebrides - smartly disguising her own treasonable action.

 'And you, Black Witch, throw out some of your own forked lightning after her!' added Lundy, brandishing her ladle.

 Viking flung over the battlements some newly-forged Advanced Thunder; Biscay was forced to back it up with her freshly-trained Force 8 Winds.

 But instead of following this with a range of gleaming lightning strokes, the Black Witch fled up to her Turret.

 And her power was greater than theirs. Using every skill she possessed, she arranged it so that the very impact of the great storm pushed her escaping sky-rider along even faster than before.

 Steadily throughout the rest of the night, Hebrides worked, hoping her escaped prisoner was safe. German Bight was more important to her than the White Witch's death.

Then, utterly overwrought, she dragged herself to GB's Study and locked them both inside to wait for his release.

She watched in disgust as the pitiful man cradled the stupid picture of her rival on the 'Weather or Not' cover. 'Will the White Witch keep her word?' she wondered as she sank into an exhausted sleep.

Surprised by a sudden strengthening wind, the fleeing Mermaid found she was being considerably helped in her efforts to swim. Viking's storm was pushing her with currents of enormous speed right to Mumbles, then Land's End, ready for her to turn left and slice towards Beaufort.

The British Isles, too, were startled by this sudden storm, after having none at all. Once again, Mr. Allbright's abilities to predict the weather were questioned, until he grew quite frantic.

But, the storm hurtled Finisterre/Fitzroy in the Fog Funnel bearing them through the night south towards Sunny Intervals and, to give him his due, Fitzroy helped balance and control them inside the Fog-funnel as it screamed along, with the raging storm pushing behind.

When they reached the White Witch's Residence, they found themselves shot rudely from the front of the Funnel's spout to land clumsily on her cloud-lawn. Flocks of Foul Weather-Birds, still clamouring and squabbling over this new-found deserted territory, rose up shrieking with fright as its true owner returned.

Wailing and lamenting, they fled back to Heligoland, leaving both nests and flapping fledglings behind.

Finisterre lay quiet, puffed out until the spinning had unspun itself and the storm had abated. She stared at the remaining strands of her spent Fog-Funnel drifting off to wreath around her sturdy towers, which had remained unshaken by the Funnel's arrival. But the dawn light revealed that her beautiful cloud-lawn lay trashed all around where she'd fallen.

Hearing her Curlews call miserably through the haze, Finisterre summoned them to clear up her ruined lawn and build themselves new nests. She felt utterly over-blown as she stumbled towards her front door. Opening it by using her Unlocking Spell, she immediately put her wand to re-charge. To her delight, Finisterre found Kittiwake – with a friend – perched on the heated towel-rail. 'She must have got in through a sky-light,' she thought.

Below them, in the centre of one of her colossal sponges, was a level nest made from cotton-buds, flannels - and a little of her best French underwear. Inside the nest a pale buff egg with lovely brown speckles had been newly laid.

'Oh Kittiwakes, I'm so pleased for you. Well done.' Finisterre was touched.

'Kittiwakes have guarded your home for you,' they chorused.

'Thank you, dear Kittiwakes. And please will you kindly wake me just before dawn breaks. I need to have a little rest for the remainder of the night - quite urgently.'

Finisterre first prepared herself a hot comforting bath, heated from her Solar panels. Into this, she poured a great deal of iodized sea-salts, and set another colossal sea-sponge afloat on its surface.

Afterwards, she fell into her Oyster-bed for a recovering sleep.

'Kitti-will-wake. Kitty-will-wake,' the Kittiwakes called, before settling down below her steamy bathroom rail.

Back at Heligoland Hall, the Toad Paperweight had watched over German Bight and Hebrides intently throughout that terrible night.

Then, just as dawn broke, a loud croak brought them both awake in time to see German Bight's hand drop open to let the stupid magazine fall to the floor; and he looked up to see the Black Witch and his Toad, both with tears running down their cheeks.

'So, my Sister, the White Witch, kept her word, and must have been able to re-charge her wand enough to undo the spell on the *'Weather or Not'* magazine. At last, my GB, you've been freed from her power.'

Now the Black Witch had foggy lights play skillfully around her hair, and her seaweedy gown appeared to glow, as magnetic forces drew German Bight towards her.

'What a fool I've been. Forgive me, Hebrides? I beg you,' he implored.

With savage eyes and powers irresistible, Hebrides took full advantage of the situation. She proposed to him, and was accepted.

At last she had him entirely for her own.

The Toad croaked persistently, trying to go with them. But the Black Witch left the Study without the creature, luring only GB up to her Turret. Here, she locked her door tightly behind them, by fastening it with a strong Black Witch's Spell.

Chapter 21
A Special Wartime Grace:

Only Malin took no part in the storm. He'd spent that entire night painting the walls, ceiling, furniture and floor of his Master Bedroom with tar. For Breakfast, he emerged from a cold bath dressed formally. Surely their new Leader would announce him Second - in-Command? He looked a lot younger since slicking some oil through his hair to make it go dark brown.

He'd come down extra early in order to search for the wrecked body of the White Witch, which should have been hurled by now on to the battlements after Viking's colossal storm.

Instead, he was greeted by an unaccustomed brightness, which flooded the Hall ... revealing that their beloved tarry slick had broken up, dispersed by the storm-waves ... and had left.

Viking sauntered down with his breastplate polished - also ready to be appointed Second-in-Command. Biscay followed closely, sporting a pair of spats starched white from various calcareous deposits found at the bottom of the Irish Sea. (Surely Hebrides would want to choose another woman as her Deputy, wouldn't she?)

Sole stayed as she always was: solefully wringing her hands.

Unfortunately, just before Lundy served Breakfast, all the Foul Weather-Birds expelled from the White Witch's lawn, returned to Heligoland, squawking news that the White Witch had escaped safely to Sunny Intervals.

'I know who let the White Witch go!' shouted Malin. 'It has to be Bight. He's the one with the key to the dungeon, isn't he? And he's meant to be here with the finished Equation as our New Leader promised. Perhaps he did carry out that proposal of marriage to Finisterre as he intended? Has he given her some of the oil, then escaped with her to Sunny Intervals I wonder? We all saw how besotted he was with her during the Feast.'

'By Boreas!' Viking swore. 'Let's all go down to his Study and see.'

They found German Bight's Study door swinging open and empty. His almost-completed Equation had been rubbed off the board, and only his Toad Paperweight sat there, glaring with frustrated eyes.

'He's gone!' Viking roared.

Malin smiled beneath his icy countenance: at last he'd rid himself of his rival.

But to their huge annoyance, German Bight hadn't left at all. For just as they got back to the Dining Hall, he entered arm in arm with Hebrides; and in his hand was the finished Equation.

Their Leader immediately appointed him Second-in-Command for completing it successfully - and on time.

Malin felt further demoralized and humiliated later that day, when Bight swaggered in to Lunch, declaring he'd already managed to translate the Equation's symbols into something quite stupendous for their War.

'I have our Battle Strategy all worked out! Gather round!'

Using his whale-bone cane, Bight bound onto the table and, picking his way smartly around various tarred and salted fish-skeletons, organized plates in close Battle Formations, using knives, forks and spoons to illustrate vantage positions.

Malin felt at first frustrated by Bight's tactics – then further annoyed as he saw his unfinished plate of Sea-Squirt Pie being used as a secret weapon.

But the others were properly astounded, and applauded his brilliance … except for Lundy, who looked on helplessly as her carefully laid Wartime Meal disintegrated into a War-zone.

'War can now be waged,' announced their new Leader, proudly … 'From now on, you're all to work flat on out on forming the Equations' Cabalistic symbols into actual War Weather.

Over the following days, Biscay not only practiced creating powerful winds, but also had her Feathered Force in peak fighting condition; while Viking's hammer continually rang like a drum-roll on the anvil, piling up violent Thunderbolts and lightning ready for War.

Sole's Header Tanks were brimming full; Malin ground out endless heavily-laden grey clouds through the rollers, ready to be inflated when required.

This Extreme Weather was stacked into order by German Bight. Soon they could declare War once everything was finalized.

Biscay eagerly took on *'Raising Morale'*, by pasting with fish-glue Wartime

Bulletins around the whole Castle:

'Don't be lazy. Stop that slacking.
Make more wind and send them packing.'

But when she pasted *'Blitz and Blizzards create hazards,'* onto Lundy's Kitchen door, following this with *'Iron Rations form Foul Passions',* the Cook was furious. She huffed like a subsiding soufflé and tore them down to make spills to light the Kitchen fire. She was not compromising her cooking to fit in with any *'War Morals'*.

Unfortunately, when Biscay returned later from drilling her Foul Feathered Force, she caught Lundy preserving some of those wholesome troops in aspic.

'Lundy, this will not do. All Foul Weather-Birds are being trained as spies or fighters. From now on it's to be Iron Rations.' Her small whip was making practiced threats towards cutting into Lundy's Kitchen table.

'I will try to make all this iron stuff then,' the Cook quickly promised, spreading her arms behind her to protect her beloved table. 'Even though my little Windy's not here to help.'

And Supper preparations saw the Foul cook thumbing tearfully through 'Wretched ways with Wartime Cookery'.

That evening, a new, harder, chastened Lundy served the evening meal. Her face had a severe Wartime look about it … and to her credit, Iron Rations of every kind filled the Dining Hall – all without her Little Helper's aid:

Hard Tack was stacked in toast racks; Sea-Biscuits layered in shallow dishes; 'Snoek' served as a dip; Scurvy-grass Salad overfilled gigantic bowls.

Lundy was 'Making Do.'

Wearing a new fighting headscarf depicting a Low destroying a High in blanket stitch, Biscay rose to say a special Wartime Grace:

Let our Ice-cap rather neatly
Cover Croydon up completely.
Having buried every car
From Aylesbury to Potters Bar.
A ton of snow will look quite pretty
Dumped on Welwyn Garden City.
Let our icebergs freeze the jeans

Off all the lads in Milton Keynes.
Give them something wet and dull
Down from York to Solihull.
And let our whirlwinds really scare
The folk in Western Super Mare.

Give the Irish and their bogs
Years of squelchyness and Fogs.
Grant them chilblains on their hands
In Wales and the Welsh Borderlands.
May The North and Scots catch flu;
Kneecaps turn a nasty blue.
May we win the Weather War,
Ruling Britain evermore.
Help us work up violent passions
To devour our Wartime Rations.

She sat down amidst thunderous applause, and they all dutifully pitched into their food like soldiers at the last meal before battle.

It was the last peace-time weather they'd have.

Part 6

Chapter 22
The Black Mermaiden

Wendy heard the enchanting sea-song first when she looked out in the early morning through the Beaufort Nursery window, where she'd been kept under the supervision of Nanny Dover. It was the same haunting lullaby her mother used to sing to her when she was little, and it made her smile sadly.

Everyone at Beaufort Castle had waited, petrified, during the night, when an unexpectedly violent storm from Heligoland had rocked the very foundations of their battlements - proving that the Foul Weather-Makers hadn't been subdued at all.

The children grew fractious and cried. Nanny said some prayers.

'Mr Allbright's been fired', said Fastnet, out of breath, as she rushed from the cloud computer with her news. 'The British Isles have been thoroughly startled by the storm, coming so suddenly after experiencing no weather at all. They're going to think up new ways of predicting the weather using an array of computers!'

'Quiet, Fastnet! Sshh! Listen! I can hear something!'

Fisher, with his keen hearing, left the Dining-room, and went to lean over the cloud-edge. 'Listen! It's '*Sweet and High*', he said in rather an out-of-breath voice. 'Can't you hear it?' With his equally keen eyesight, Fisher had spotted a black speck, singing way down in the choppy sea-waves far below.

Fisher yelled up at King Faeroes' window; 'The Mermaiden's back!'

Faeroes gave a whoop of joy. Bounding from his bed, he whistled up a Wind- Force from the stables. On it he dived down to sea-level, veering dangerously from left to right, until he'd located his singing wife. He was over the moon to see her again, and swept the slimy creature up in his arms … a little amazed to be carrying a black wife back to his Castle.

'What an admirable disguise,' Fastnet remarked, wondering at Fair Isle's dark appearance.

'Really huge storm-waves pushed me back here in record time,' the Mermaiden gasped, dripping with oily sea-water.

Nanny Dover sighed with relief. Although the Castle Battlements were a little shaky after the storm, every inhabitant was now safe … and Fair Isle's return would restore King Faeroes' power. The children clapped with glee and, encircling their Queen, danced around her in a ring. Nanny Dover smiled. 'Everything's going to be alright.'

'But where's the Foul Earthling?' Fair Isle suddenly demanded. 'What've you done with her? Finisterre said she'd probably be here? Bring her to me at once.'

Wendy was quickly ushered into the Dining-room, where she stepped forward from Nanny's protection, staring at this wondrous sight: a beautiful black Mermaid. She was highly impressed.

To their amazement, Fair Isle gave Wendy a hug. 'You must be the Earthling Finisterre saved,' she said, once their hug had slipped apart from its oily embrace.

The other Fair Weather-Makers stood around embarrassed. They realized they'd been treating the Earthling badly.

'But there's no time to talk now,' Fair Isle panted, taking off her pink backpack and throwing it down. 'Plymouth, fetch me my needles and my coloured yarn straight away.'

Plymouth hurried off, frowning, but did as she was bid.

'Why in the Skies is she wanting to knit now,' laughed Forties.

But then everyone at Beaufort gathered around to watch an amazing spectacle take place. Wendy sat down on a cloud-mound near the Mermaid, and watched the proceedings with relief. She was waiting for an opportunity to ask about Finisterre.

Settling herself comfortably into a piece of puffy cloud, Fair Isle cast on many stitches. Then, once her breathing was back to its normal rhythm, she turned to face due South-East - towards Sunny Intervals – and, concentrating hard, allowed her eyes to glaze over.

For some moments she waited, then …

All at once, her needles began to click; and, growing oily from the tar, raced along at fantastic speed. In front of Fair Isle, a massive scarf poured from the needles. It looked like a map, for it bore strange information; knitted - as it was decoded from her mind - in clever Fair Isle designs and unusually bright colours.

Everyone watched awe-struck until the Mermaiden, finishing the final row, cast off neatly in plain and purl. 'This is the Cabalistic Equation,' she explained, glowing with pride. 'It will give us Heligoland's War Weather Strategy. It comes via KR Magnetic 2 from Finisterre. With it, we'll be able to form some good Positions of Defence.'

'You mean Finisterre's alive!' Wendy clapped with joy. Fisher, too, beamed and did a little cloud-dance with the happy Earthling, while the children laughed even louder.

And at last their Castle atmosphere was restored.

'I thought the Black Witch was going to kill her,' Wendy explained.

'You see, Finisterre risked her life to save mine, sending me safely away, while she was being overcome by Hebrides. I'd do anything to see her and thank her.'

'Well, she'd certainly be pleased at your recovery.' Fair Isle was astonished at the Earthling's Fair looks: hair long and sleek, a face now glowing with health - 'How did you manage it?'

Nanny stepped forward. 'I just carried on giving her Ambrosia … and although at first she wanted to return to Heligoland … now, as you can see, she radiates virtue and good intent. She's even been useful; I got her singing rousing songs to keep our children's spirits up, then got her sweeping Gloomy Fog from the Nursery when it formed too thick. I've even taught her the basics of Fair Weather-making …'

Wendy decided to say nothing about the way they'd treated her before, and with her new Fair, forgiving nature, enjoyed the Mermaiden's Fine Praise.

Wizard Wight, particularly quiet, stood, guiltily, behind the others.

'Then is Finisterre definitely on our side?' Fastnet persisted. 'We need to know, urgently.'

'Well she is … and she isn't,' said Fair Isle, cautiously. 'She did look more than a little Foul when I saw her. She told me there was a lot to do first: make herself fit ... get things back in proportion … but now, if you'll excuse me, I have to make everyone Breakfast.'

And that's when everything at Beaufort Castle changed.

The Mermaiden carried her backpack into the larder, spied the tins of Sardines in Brine, bent out the corners of each, emptied out the brine – poured in a large dessertspoonful of tar. 'This will get them all back to work,' she grinned.

'Breakfast's ready,' she sang in a high, inviting treble.

Barely moments after swallowing the Sardines in Oil, Highly disturbing things began to happen to every Weather-Maker:

King Faeroes' eyes turned from their usual turquoise to a glow of startling emerald green. His voice, too, swelled to something more vital, more aggressive, as he stood to say: 'Now that my Mermaiden's back, let's make Weather that'll heat up the whole of Britain, bathing it in perpetual sunshine.'

'Create a line of dust-devils right across Salisbury Plain,' ventured Forties.

'A whirling mass of thermals over the Chiltern Hills,' Fastnet trilled, her eyes gleaming magenta.

'Turn Scotland into a desert,' Fisher suggested, his eyes blazing bright green.

'Bring in a nasty side-wind for the Oxford and Cambridge Boat-Race?' giggled Plymouth, her eyes blazing an anemone-blue.

'Set an adverse current and choppy breeze for the Henley Regatta' added Dogger.

'Inches of seriously-warm water covering Ireland,' laughed Bailey.

'Very hot winds sweeping across Wales …' the children joined in.

Fair Isle grinned, smearing her apron with streaks of tar.

'Definitely some vicious sunspots in Swindon.' Wizard Wight's eyes fizzled brightest of all: for this stuff was giving them exactly the power he'd been searching for. The Earthling Girl was now irrelevant. Yes, he could ignore her altogether.

Wendy, though, was staring, thoroughly confused: this wasn't the kind of Fair Weather she'd been learning from Nanny Dover - surely? What they were suggesting was exceptionally strong stuff – admittedly it still excited her a little

– but Wendy had not been allowed any of the oily sardines herself: she was still being held on her strict diet of Ambrosia creamed rice.

'Hey! Wait!' Fair Isle shouted. 'Calm! Calm! Finisterre made me tell you to employ only Positions of Defence in return for relaying this Equation to us. If we disobey, she probably won't be helping at all.'

149

The others looked disappointed, but had to agree. Although Fair Isle, herself, felt even more exhilarated by the oil, she remained sensible enough to know they'd be unlikely to win any Weather War without the White Witch's help … but then she remembered that Hebrides had taken away her wand - so how could she help them without it? Her heart sank. We're going to have to do it all on our own.

Later, from a vantage point on the Long Gallery, Nanny Dover grinned; Finisterre's advice was holding true. She'd disliked the tarry sardines, and only had a small helping herself. But to her amazement, the Dining-room table had been carried into the Central Courtyard and was now covered in a green baize cloth, where felt clouds, stuck to the ends of curled-up sardine tin tops, were pushed at High Pressure - endlessly back and forth - showing different ideas for their Lines of Defence.
'Meals will become more informal affairs now, without a Dining-room table', she sighed.
'Well, maybe this oily pollution is a good idea,' the Mermaiden thought. 'It's certainly got them working again and roused into a proper Warlike spirit - exactly as I'd intended.'

Up inside his Turret, Wizard Wight, Professor of Fine Celestial Arts, now worked fast. With this New Strength, he could at last use the Tome's workings … could form brilliant stuff. But within this Tome he'd discovered certain Cabalistic combinations very much stronger than mere Defence …
'Yes! Combinations capable of allowing Beaufort to Win a Weather War.'
The Wizard sat back and grinned. The power he'd lacked before had, like a magic gift, been brought to him by their clever Mermaiden.
Nevertheless … he'd still keep a keen Weather-eye on that Earthling girl. There was still something about her he didn't quite trust.

Later that day, when it was Fastnet's turn to make High Tea, she discovered the remains of Fair Isle's stash of 'special oil'. Now Fastnet really liked what the tar was doing - especially to herself: she was no longer the thin, stringy Fair Weather-Maker – no, she was now more filled out; bulging with muscle – and it felt Really Good. So, secretly, she tipped the rest of the oil into their sardine soup.

Afterwards, everyone - except Wendy - looked almost out of control. They reminded her strongly of her own disreputable state reflected in the large kitchen pan at Heligoland Hall when she was there. And during a special War Meeting that King Faeroes held after the meal was over, Wendy realized that something very dangerous was occurring. But she felt powerless to help.

'I vote we bake the whole of Britain in pretty High-Level Sunstroke,' Plymouth suggested, her eyes violet and swivelling. 'Very High Pressure everywhere!'

'We could melt icebergs in South-East Iceland, and blow them down South.' Fastnet's mousy hair bounced, taking on some stunning purple streaks.

'Evaporate every single grey cloud while we're at it,' added Forties, rearing up.

'Get our Fair Weather-birds to peck theirs to death!' Dogger squirmed in his seat at the delicious thought.

'Why don't we evaporate all the Foul Weather-Makers?' Bailey's hair had risen into a spectacular electrified frizz. 'Then there'd be no opposition at all.'

'Why not go further still? Warm up France, Belgium, Germany, Scandinavia ... maybe even across the ocean to the USA!' Fisher's muscles ached with sudden growth. He visualised great magnetic storms raging: deserts completely covering Asia, with dry, waterless earth.

The Wizard's eyes smouldered as he watched. He rose from his chair, and holding his staff aloft, shouted, 'Good! This is much more like what I had in mind. 'And I have to tell you all that I know exactly how we can manufacture all this **Extreme Weather**... and right away.'

'Well done, Wizard Wight!' Faeroes exclaimed.

'Wait! You realize it'll mean changing all the settings on my Cloud Machine,' Forties interrupted, 'if I'm to deliver this Tropical stuff.'

'Mustn't grumble, Forties,' Plymouth warned, a double halo of static floating above her hair.

'And I'll need to crank up all our measuring devices for recording these new Extremes,' added Fisher.

'We can do this,' Fastnet encouraged.

'Hotter and Hotter! Hotter and Hotter!'

Suddenly the children piped up, startling them all.

Their eyes were popping out of their heads and had turned the colour of soot.

Fair Isle realized she'd forgotten that the children ate what they'd been eating; now she felt fully responsible for their condition. And although she herself felt surprisingly wicked, the Mermaid began to wonder if it had been such a good idea to bring along the tar? All their eyes looked wilder, so out of control, so unnatural. Her own dark scales had even taken on a spectacular oily iridescence during the night. But the dose had definitely been far too much for the children … They were now both hyperactive. 'Is Pollution really the right course to take?' she wondered. 'What have I done?'

All day long – and the next – and the next, the Fair Weather-Makers worked eagerly, piling up Extreme Weather; storing it behind Cloud-cover.

Then, troubling news was winged in by a flock of Fair Weather Gannets, who delivered their Bulletin in loud staccato-stabs, as if they'd been diving for oily fish. And what they told heated the Castle's War-plans almost to boiling-point:

'Captain Humber is expired Craak! – the Black Witch leads them now!'

'They're creating War Weather fast under her command.'

'Finisterre's escaped back to Sunny Intervals. Craak!'

'Inside the Black Witch's own Fog-Funnel!'

'Get ready to wage War straight away! Craak!'

'What! You mean Hebrides actually helped her escape?' Forties was dumb-founded.

'Yes! Craak! Craak! And you have to warn the British Isles what's up!'

'The White Witch says so. Craak!'

Their news delivered, they flew off in V-formation.

'Good Heavens! Why would Hebrides help Finisterre escape – if it didn't mean Finisterre was now on their side at Sunny Intervals?' A puzzled expression overcast Faeroes' face.

'Oh, I didn't want to tell you,' Fair Isle suddenly broke down sobbing. 'She told me herself they were to release her in return for finishing the Equation that German Bight had nearly completed. Presumably she managed the swap.'

'She'd never help them like that!' Fisher exploded … Never!' But all at once, he felt even less sure – the two Witches were, after all, he remembered, Sisters … weren't they? This news was even worse.

'Then we'll need to wage War as soon as we can – however, it'll be without the White Witch's help,' Faeroes announced. 'Away, and get on with making Extreme Weather for the rest of the day.'

At day's end, Faeroes called them in from work. He stood at the head of the Dining-room table in the Courtyard, looking almost out of control. He'd eaten more of the oily sardines than anyone else – through being almost starved over his long days of mourning for his wife.

'Listen, everyone!' he gesticulated wildly. 'Quieten down! Today I've been formulating an excellent plan: I've decided what we are to do can be easily expanded. We're to call it **Global Warming**. A new idea, never thought of before!'

Everyone was startled by this; Wizard Wight thought the idea stunning.

'Yes!' continued their King. 'There'll be exciting new weather types: erratic, sneaky stuff – violent goings on - things we've never tried before: flash floods, freak waves, Tornadoes … even Hurricanes ... everywhere.

'I mean to alter the whole Weather System completely. We'll need to make lots more Extreme stuff, of course, but it could be soon … sooner than you think. What's more, I've decided that to fight this Weather War … Yes, first we'll use the Defensive Positions against Heligoland that Fair Isle knitted into her scarf … but it'll be merely to fool the enemy and appease the White Witch.

Behind these Defences, our new Extreme Weather will be stacked ready to use. So we shall attack them first,' he shouted – 'and after that, WIN!'

'You mean really have Fair Weather Forever'?' Nanny Dover asked, querulously. 'What an idea!'

'Fair Weather Forever! Fair Weather Forever!' chanted the frantic children.

'Fair-ocious Weather,' giggled Fastnet, quite beside herself.

Faeroes smiled crookedly as he stepped down from the table.

'Then we will work even throughout the nights, if necessary … for I have a final piece of information to give: I'm informing you all, that once we've enough of this different weather manufactured, I'm sending the Great Fulmer to flap off to Heligoland carrying … 'A Declaration of War.'

Fair Isle was relieved. Now that Beaufort could make Extreme Weather, they might, after all, be able to win without needing Finisterre's help.

But Wendy, however, was seriously alarmed. This kind of Weather certainly wasn't what Finisterre meant them to make. She was really scared now with everything happening in the sky, and although she felt both Fair and, deeper down, still a little Foul … she was aware that her Grandfather's Tome must encourage its reader to wage war - not prevent it. And now it was doing the same to Wizard Wight. This sticky, polluting tar, giving them all such power, would lead only to massive disaster - everywhere on Earth.

The whole Castle had completely changed, Wendy realized - taken complete leave of its senses. She found herself standing on her chair, shouting out:

'And I have something important to add! Finisterre's quite right: Britain has to be warned immediately – before any Weather War takes place. I insist.'

And she stamped her foot down hard.

'Hush! Hush! Earthling,' Wizard Wight soothed, 'here is my idea: I know exactly how to warn the British Isles … satisfying both yours, Wendy, and the White Witch's demands.' He stood grandly before them, smiling crookedly.

'Once we've made enough of this new type of Fine Weather, you're all invited to sit out on the battlements in the early evening to attend a great Sky Spectacle - a Weather-Warning, just before we fight. It's to be called my **'Fantastic Light Show.'**

At last, here was a way for Wendy to escape. Wizard Wight's event would make an excellent opportunity both for her to get back her Grandfather's Tome and leave. The Wizard would be away, setting up the sky.

Then, instantly, this second opportunity was dashed - for the Wizard added: 'But no-one's to interrupt me in my Turret while I make my preparations. Is that clear?'

There was nothing for it: Wendy would have to get the Tome while they were at the Show itself; steal in to the Wizard's vacant Turret, take it safely back to … to … where? Nowhere seemed safe up here any more …

…. However, there was another way … why not carry it down to Earth.

Yes, Earth … and into the keeping of Mr Allbright, as her Grandfather had instructed. Although Mr Allbright had been fired, he'd know exactly how to destroy the Tome without anyone else having to know about it. Into his hands was the right place for it to be. She'd ride down on Finisterre's Mare; leave the sky altogether.

By doing that, then none of these Weather-Makers could use Grandfather's Tome.

Chapter 23
The Fantastic Light Show

Inside his Turret, the Professor of Fine Celestial Arts worked fast. He had every chest flung open, startling his astral orbs, sending heavenly bodies clashing overhead as he pulled out and threw around himself all the old-fashioned magical bits of weather, now no longer of any use to them.

All their new Extreme stuff was being stacked, Cloud-covered, well behind Beaufort Castle's towering Cumulus.

Wendy prepared how she would leave. She watched carefully.

First, she discovered where Wizard Wight kept a spare Turret key … in one of her empty Ambrosia creamed Rice tins, on the highest Kitchen shelf.

Next, she prepared a visit to Forties' workshop and found that, while a new, heavier windlass was being installed to haul out their new heavier type of War Clouds, his old windlass had been thrown into a corner. She carried this to Finisterre's Backing Wind, and led it gently, but secretly, behind some fluff at the very edge of the lawn. There, she tethered it, using the windlass. Next, she hid her backpack under cloud-cover nearby, ready to smuggle the Tome away inside.

Just as it was beginning to get dark, and preparations for the Fantastic Light Show were completed, the Wizard charged the inhabitants of Beaufort to sit in a line, with their legs (Fair Isle and little Thames with their fish-tails) dangling over the Battlements.

Now the Wizard swirled his cloak about his shoulders to gain their attention. 'Are you all ready?'

'Yes', they cried excitedly. 'Begin! Begin!'

'For my Sky Show, I've chosen to use up all the old weather we won't be needing any longer. This'll be quite adequate to give as Wendy's Earth Warning – but, of course, not powerful enough now, compared to the new stuff we've been preparing.'

The Show began with the Wizard making an opening gesture to get the atmosphere right.

By extending a layer of Stratus cloud over the horizon, and shimmering the thinnest amount of Cirrostratus above to act as a backdrop, he created a sunset, which glowed softly around an ascending moon. Then, by adding more haze to his palette, made distant clouds appear goldeny-yellow, then orange, then dimming to a gentle red. Everyone applauded.

Wendy, who was sitting at the end of the row, quietly slipped away at this point.

She fetched the key from the empty Ambrosia tin in the larder, ran up the steps to the Wizard's Turret, and unlocked the door.

Most of the room's contents had been used for his Show, but there, under the strange dangling orbs, was Grandfather's large purple Tome, lying in the bottom of an empty chest. As she picked it up, it reverted immediately to a pleasant green in her hands. She carried this down the steps, over the lumpy Cumulus, and along to Finisterre's Wind-Force.

She'd be ready to leave for Earth straight away.

Around her, the sky was flashing in all kinds of lurid hues; the air filled with sharp sparks of dancing scintillation from the Wizard's Show. They spread running lines of dots over the Tome's cover... which was when she found herself overcome with an overwhelming compulsion to look inside ... just once again.

As she opened its heavy age-old cover, she found, to her amazement, that she now understood many of the Weather-symbols - unlike when she'd last opened it sitting up in bed so long ago at home.

Carefully, she turned the parchment pages, discovering they'd been written as the result of century after century of accumulated Weather-Lore from Persia, Egypt, the Far East: India, Turkey, China ... Who'd written it all? How had Johann Heinrich Lambert collected it all together? Translated it into Cabalistic symbols? And why was it so powerful?

Soon it was drawing her into its secrets ... captivating ... tantalizing ... pushing information outwards from every page ... worming ideas into her mind. Telling her that if she could only just concentrate on the strange symbols even more, its Weather-Lore could speak to her; instruct her how to look for further interesting combinations ... how, using these together, might be intensely pleasing ... would allow her endless power ...

157

Only then did Wendy fully understand that the Tome must change according to whoever held it in their hands. So that's why Grandfather was so frantic to have it kept in 'safe hands'; he must've known that all along. But why hadn't he managed to destroy the Tome? Did he not have the power to do so? And, above all, how did he resist its power himself?

Her eyes filled with sudden tears as she remembered Grandpa - the Earth ... her home. How she longed now to be back with her Mother and her friends. Her falling tears fizzed and evaporated quickly, preventing her from reading further ... and

CLUNK! She snapped the Tome closed. The tears for home had been enough to stop her reading.

She was strong – She would not be fooled. Her Grandfather must have been strong as well.

She pushed the Tome into the backpack, swung this over her shoulders - and was about to unhitch the windlass to make her escape, when ... 'Wendy! Wendy!'

She whipped round ...

And here was Nanny Dover, stumbling towards her, calling breathlessly, 'Here you are! Are you all right? The Wizard really wants to know where you are.'

Nanny Dover had Wendy's bowl of Ambrosia in one hand and a Weather-proof folded over the other. 'I've been sent to find you during the Interval,' she puffed. 'They need you now, dear. You're to be their Look-Out ... chosen by Wizard Wight to be sent to a position of safety, high in the sky - once the show is over.'

'I asked them to keep you safe from the War, you see. High Above will be nicely out of the way. Fisher's lending you his *Absolutely Weatherproof* so you won't feel any cold ... none at all. Come on, quickly. Put it on. You've got to leave right after the Weather-Warning Show is over – So eat this, dear, while we walk - to keep you going for later.'

And Wendy could not, would not, disobey the person who'd cared for her so well. Thankfully, Fisher's 'Absolutely Weatherproof' puffed up around her with its brilliant Cloud-fluff insulation, hiding the backpack neatly as they returned to the ramparts. Why had she been so slow? Had the Tome deliberately held her back?

As she went along eating, Wendy wondered, too, whether Finisterre had found time to look inside the Tome herself before racing onto the rocks at Heligoland to battle with the Black Witch? If she had, would that have been long enough for her to be influenced by it? The Tome, where the White Witch had flung it down, had shone a bright glowing gold under her hands. Surely that Fair colour proved Finisterre would use its knowledge wisely? But had she been meaning to escape with it to Sunny Intervals in order to keep it safe? Or use it herself?

'Ah! There you are, Wendy. Now we can continue.'

The Wizard's eyes were blazing – but filled also with unease - as he fixed them onto her. He needed her here, where he could keep a watch on her. Was she, perhaps, still after his Tome, he wondered?

Nanny settled her down by her side, then signalled the Wizard to continue with the second half of his Show.

…'And now, with my Art of Wizardry, and powers of Defraction, Refraction and Interference … by borrowing light from the Sun and Moon … I announce my

'Luminous Phenomena' in three parts.'

With further sweeping movements and clever manipulation of ice-crystals in the upper atmosphere, the Magician formed Corona, Iridescence, Halo phenomena and special Glory. Then, with the aid of water droplets, produced wondrous Mirages, Shimmer, and further Scintillation.

The show drew to a close with an array of roseate twilight colours sinking Westwards, and flourishing greeny-blue waves of Northern Lights – also a sprinkling of Crepuscular rays – Nanny's favourite bit of weather.

Faeroes stood up, still clapping. 'That'll be all we'll ever see of these archaic weather-types. So now, after we've first pushed forward our Lines of Defence …. all we need do next in order to win … is to set in motion our **Extreme Weather Conditions.'**

Everyone clapped again, as their mild, gentle, normal kind of weather faded silently and sadly down beyond the horizon.

It was the last peace-time weather they'd have.

Part 7
The War of the Weather

Chapter 24
Warm Front and Cold Front

Skeins of Fair Weather-Birds, flocking in their hundreds, winged towards the safety of Beaufort Castle, forming white-arrowed lines like Clouds of moving snow below an unhappy sky.

They heralded a red dawn of awesome proportion.

Beyond Beaufort, the skies were unsafe, filled with the Foul Feathered Force, wheeling in swarm-bursts of swirling mass.

But the Fair Weather-Makers were ready … so were piles of unusual hot unsettling weather, hidden well behind Beaufort Castle.

At 06.00 hours Greenwich Mean Time, the people of Britain looked up, to see the blood-streaked dawn drawn right across the sky.

People in the towns and suburbs marvelled; never had they seen such strange weather happenings without any reason.

'The sky is showing us one thing – then another. The weather's never been so erratic. What does it all mean - after having none at all?'

'It's like the weather's tipping over and showing us a bit of everything as it goes.'

'Is it our fault, perhaps? Is there anything we should have been doing?'

Before long, the hair on their scalps prickled; the hackles on their pets rose, too; – and some howling could be heard.

Something in the atmosphere was definitely not right for man nor beast.

Those who knew about 'The Weather' had already heeded the extraordinary fluctuating sky-warnings the night before ... especially after Fair Isle had quickly added a multi-coloured halo round the moon – foretelling rain, and after that, a mackerel sky - signalling the ordinary approach of thundery weather. She knew this would be more acceptable to sailors and farmers than Wizard Wight's psychedelics.

The sailors and farmers did understand: the sailors made for land; the farmers rushed about bringing in cattle and sheep, and tying loose things down.

The Shipping Forecast, too, predicted an abundance of weather in every sea area … *"Viking, Forties, Forth Tyne, Dogger, Bailey; Low; winds veering South-West to West - then North-West. Visibility poor, two miles. Hebrides,*

Malin, Irish Sea: becoming cyclonic, wintry showers, locally poor. German Bight, Sole; 6 or 7, gale-force winds, becoming severe 9 ... 10 ... 11 ... ... no, possibly 12 ... "

The Met Office, in complete confusion, predicted - with the aid of several new computers - practically everything that morning ... just to make sure.

Heeding the forecast, people got out parasols, then umbrellas, then swimming costumes, then sou'westers, balaclavas and gloves.

At Heligoland Hall that morning, Malin came downstairs eagerly and early. He'd slept badly, due to some strange flickering lights around them in the sky. The remains of it lit up an aerogram from Beaufort lying on the sea-weed-strangled mat. It was a Declaration of War ... and the Foul Weather-Makers' weren't quite ready. Malin roared.

As a 'Look-Out' for Beaufort, Wendy, wearing Fisher's *'Absolutely Weatherproof'*, had been launched from the Beaufort battlements and was now blown right up into the Cirrostratus to "a position of neutrality."
She cowered inside a small puffy cloud expertly sponged together by Forties. It was half way between grey and white to camouflage its occupant. Her job was to let Beaufort know when the enemy approached.

Wendy felt truly trapped. She knew that, soon enough, Wizard Wight would discover she'd stolen his Tome and hidden it somewhere at Beaufort. He'd be needing it after they won, in order to continue creating their Extreme Weather. 'I must keep calm, while I think about what to do,' she told herself.

Then she thought: 'Why don't I just jettison the Tome into the sea below, rather than into Mr Allbright's hands?'

... That was before she remembered how her tears had mysteriously fizzled, simply refusing to sink into the paper. The book was obviously completely unaffected by water, and would merely float back to land.

She sat on her cloud feeling sad and hopeless; all her chances of escape vanished into thin air. Her small cloud hadn't been persuaded to carry her away from it all by veering with her suddenly down to Earth ... it was "more than its fluff was worth".

Already the sky around Wendy was changing: an unsettling eerie yellow light seemed to glow from everywhere at once. And when a fitful wild, biting wind blew up, she poked her head out of her cloud. … And what she saw was terrifying!

On one side, far below her, the Warm Front had formed.
It boasted large white Defence Clouds, strongly billowing.

On the other side, still far away, a Cold Front, packed with menacing black clouds, shifted awkwardly to and fro as it attempted to organize itself.

Immediately below Wendy, was an extraordinary positioning of Fair Sea-Birds, swooping, gliding, darting, screaming …

All at once, Wendy realized that she'd been plunged right into the middle of a War Zone - and there was now nothing she could do about it.

At Beaufort, Nanny Dover blanched as she peered from a window. She saw a troubled sea thrown up all around. Running to their new Barometer, she witnessed it falling sharply. 'It has begun,' she announced, clutching the children to her - who were shivering, despite their thermal underwear. Sensibly, she hid them under the Dining-room table.

At Heligoland, no such feelings were displayed by Lundy. Fearlessly, she'd already prepared a 'Victory Soup'. Though a little premature, it had everything in it - and was exceptionally difficult to stir.

In The Cold Front, Malin-the-Bad, Commander in Chief, was ordering his Storm Troops into position in the Enemy Lines. He was still in a Foul mood from the fact they'd not been the first to declare War.

Wearing formal battle-dress, and adjusting a heavy line of medals across his chest, Malin was enough to inspire evil … which was why Hebrides, their new Leader, had chosen him to be in charge of the fighting line-up, allowing her to concentrate on getting the pressure down very Low.

Nevertheless, their Front was still not entirely ready.

Sole, out of control as usual, had let go an unnecessary amount of intermittent rain far too soon.

'Confound it, woman!' Malin snorted, 'Shape up! Get ready to advance!'

German Bight, Second-in-Command, attempted to line up the Clouds in strict order. A few looked rather thick.

'There's to be no woolly thinking in this battle!' Hebrides shrieked.

164

Viking was having difficulty spacing the isobars properly.

Hebrides was especially embarrassed by Biscay, who, in a daring Black Watch tartan with matching sneakers, marched her little bits of fluff backwards and forwards along their Lines shrilling, 'Push them back! Push them back! Push them way, way back!'

In the precisely-defined Warm Front, however, the white clouds fluffed to attention as King Faeroes-the-Good passed by, riding on a magnificent silver cloud, his crown glittering in the sunlight.

Fisher, Second-in-Command, had already checked that the wind arrows were pointing in the right direction.

Wizard Wight had selected some of his finest weather symbols to put in the Front.

Dogger spaced the Millibars in artistic, but salient positions, and Forties made sure their clouds were pressed together in a dense fluffy mass.

Only Fastnet whizzed up and down in a vaporous state: 'Finisterre's not arrived to help!' she cried. 'I hoped she'd be here; I thought she'd decide to stand by us. She really isn't on our side, is she?'

'We'll just have to start without her, or we'll lose our advantage,' shouted Plymouth. 'Look!'

For, high above them, Wendy was standing on her cloud signalling urgently that the appointed time had come.

Quickly and efficiently, Fastnet sent up a colourful array of Weather Balloons to test the humidity and temperature of the upper atmosphere. Then she raised her arm to Faeroes.

'ADVANCE!' their Leader ordered.

'No!' cried Fair Isle. 'Finisterre insisted we stand and defend. Only after that do we use our Extreme Weather waiting behind Beaufort Castle.'

'But she's not here, is she ... and I say ADVANCE,' announced Faeroes, sharply.

The Warm Front moved forward, turning Fair Isle's Defensive Equation into Attacking Mode.

At its Leading Edge, Forties and Bailey's dramatic cloud-line-up was built into a wall of powerful, intelligent layers in the following way:

165

The Top layer: feathery wisps of *Cirrus* composed of sharp, lethal ice crystals.

Beneath that: thin lines of *Cirrocumulus*, tufts of *Ucinus*, and rippling lines of *Floccus*. This group defended the upper atmosphere, forming the Light Artillery.

Directly below: great ranks of *Altostratus* pushed along *Cirrus Intortus*, tangled like barbed wire, and forming the medial position.

At the bottom edge: *Cumulus*, the heap cloud, formed the Heavy Artillery, rolling along in sparkling white luminescence, super-saturated with water-drops.

Advancing at a good pace, they gained rapidly on the enemy, moving forwards at first some Warm Winds, which rushed to and fro across their Front to confuse the opposition.

Then, at the last minute, Plymouth bravely rode out before them all to raise their morale. Unfurling the Beaufort Flag, she lifted it on High for all to see.

Inside the Cold Front, Malin was furious. Their flag, he remembered, was still ripped in two - possibly from one of Viking's tempers - the tattered remains stating 'HEL' even now locked frozen to the flagpole.

He slashed his cane through the air.

'Troops, charge at RAMMING SPEED!' he yelled.

Modest showers quickly increased to widespread rain; black clouds raced forward so fiercely that their dark shadows dappled the waves below with evil smudges.

Now, with both Fronts converging, every cloud moved rapidly, manifesting sharply-varying levels of pressure … and all much too fast.

CRASH!

The two air currents collided Head on. Riding up together, they locked tightly into an Occluded Front.

From the Bristol Channel to Cape Wrath, the battle raged in fearful deadlock. Wind arrows whizzed, weather symbols clashed; some clouds burst on impact, causing downpours. Rain fell in profusion throughout the British Isles.

Wendy clung on desperately as she found herself shot even higher from the jolting Occlusion – but not high enough to prevent a bullet of Ball Lightning to sail completely through part of her cloud.

Momentarily, her breath was knocked out of her from the impact of the shock-wave. So she was still winded when it exploded violently in an intense Fire-burst somewhere in the Warm Front beyond.

When Wendy came round - once she'd caught her breath back - she noticed that the Ball Lightning had burnt a great hole right through her cloud-fluff, causing it to lose height rapidly. It was sinking them down, down, down, straight into the fighting Sea-Birds below.

Frantically, Wendy grabbed at her cloud's disintegrating fluff, weaving it together in the way Forties had taught, packing it tightly to fill the gaping hole. Then, pulling a layer of the mended cloud over her head like a duvet, she hid beneath it waiting for the worst, while attempting to shut off the clamour of the Sea-Birds by covering her ears …

For, underneath their own Weather War, another deadly Battle of the Sea-Birds raged – Foul fighting Fair.

Sharp talons met soft feathers, curved beaks pecked at webbed feet. Shrilling, swerving, shrieking and stalling, they were battered with the force of rain so hard, that it smashed some downwards into the choppy waves below.

Then, over from the East, Wendy saw the Snow Geese in perfect V-formation wing in low over the water, making a weird honking battle-cry; their white feathers ruffled in the prevailing wind, their necks stretched forward intently.

But a counter attack came from the West, as a pack of hefty black Cormorants came skimming just above the waves, with flickering wings and cruel pecking beaks.

Soon the whole sky was alive with flocks soaring in over the horizon. Gannets dived in W's, bombing onto Razorbills below, which screeched and ducked beneath the waves.

The Earthlings on the West Coast could scarcely look in terror, as ancient fears made them cross themselves for safety.

Wendy sobbed at the sight as she continued sinking through their Battle Zone. Soon, her cloud could barely hold her up. Before long, she herself would be smashed into the waves, together with all the drowning Sea-Birds.

'Higher cloud, higher! Blow upwards!' Wendy's muffled voice urged. Bravely, she threw off her duvet cloud-covering to lighten the load.

And then, amazingly, her cloud was able to move up through their fighting zone – swiftly, effortlessly, above and away from the hideous spectacle - then it stopped short. Puzzled, Wendy peered over her cloud-edge to see why.

The wind around her had died completely because, in the Cold Front, Hebrides had moved in a layer of foggy Altostratus Opacus, so extensive that it stretched from Northumberland to the Isle of Dogs, bringing visibility down to a few feet.

There was absolute havoc: no one could see a thing. Wendy flattened herself on her back with her backpack holding her well down into the fluff as the foggy cloud pressed in. It squeezed her small cloud into ridges all around her, and there grew also a grey ghostly quietness.

Every sound was eaten by a swirling mist.

Only Wendy's own heart was heard - beating hard.

'Help!' Fair Isle called from somewhere below. 'Our whole Front's splitting into sections! What's the Cold Front up to?'

Their Warm Front had failed utterly to understand it was being undercut with cold air, forcing their hot air to mix turbulently with the cold above, first vertically, then horizontally. Eddies formed sporadically, shifting off in isolated masses of twirling wind.

'Front, ascend together!' Malin shouted suddenly. 'Try to condense! When you've cooled enough, precipitate hard!'

'That's madness! Our Front will be completely broke up!' roared Forties.

Now, thoroughly confused, the Warm Front faltered. Who should it obey? A slight kink appeared in its Leading Edge.

Faeroes, however, saw that Malin's tactics were clever.

Filled with inspiration, he dashed out heroically.

'Consider *Buys Ballot's Law*,' he urged:
"*If you find yourself confused in battle, stand with your back to the wind, then the centre of Low Pressure will always be on your left.*"
Courage! Courage!' he cried.

A cheer went up through their lines.

With renewed vigour they swept upwards.

And it worked.

From the safety of her new, higher position, Wendy witnessed the Warm Front pelting down hard onto the Cold Front, battering it mightily.

The fogged-up cloud tried to move lower, then shift to one side, but was unable to budge. Bit by bit it disintegrated until, super-saturated with water-droplets, it was pushed humiliatingly backwards over the coast.

'VICTORY!' echoed and re-echoed across the battle-sky ... cheered on by Plymouth's little bits of fluff. The Warm Front had won. And by attacking first, they'd only used up their defensive weather - managing it easily - even without Finisterre's help.

Wendy, who'd spread her arms out over her cloud's tattered remains, saw, through its holes, the Cold Front retreating fast.

However, it also revealed to her a great mass of exhausted Sea-Birds, landed in their various flocks on the Western shores of Wales.

In ragged array, they stalked the beaches, lamenting the feathered corpses already washed ashore in the great swell of the ocean. Their War was over.

Wendy sobbed at the sight. If she'd protected her Grandfather's Tome properly in the first place, none of this would have happened. Yes, it was entirely her fault that the British Weather was ruined.

In the period of stagnant mugginess that followed, Wendy, still suffering a painful wrenching in her chest from crying over the Sea-Birds' terrible plight, found that her small cloud had been floating gently downwards, and had now managed to settle onto a larger one in their victorious Warm Front.

While she recovered, Wendy snuggled inside its interior, and watched as their exhausted army cleared the skies.

Enemy Altostratus was swept into heaps. Faeroes evaporated some, others that had 'just run out of puff', he forgave, offering them positions at Beaufort, provided they shaped up and behaved in a regular way.

'Right, everyone!' their King ordered, 'now the skies are cleared, we're ready for our Extreme Weather to take effect.'

'I will prepare Earth first by allowing the Sun to startle it into sudden, shocking heat,' offered Plymouth, smiling broadly.

'Yes, a blazing 38 degrees should get things going,' suggested Bailey, beaming at their success.

Fair Isle, Fastnet and Forties clapped eagerly.

Feeling much stronger, Wendy was able to leave her depleted cloud and make her way over to join the others. Fisher, still shivering, asked for his '*Absolutely Weatherproof*' back, now that it was as all over.

… Then, as she turned to thank him for its protection, Wizard Wight spotted the Earthling's backpack … a backpack he knew had been inside his Turret, thrown into a corner. Also, whatever was inside that backpack was rather heavy … pulling her backwards … more than it should.

'She has the Tome in there!' he muttered.

But before he had time to alert the others, he felt the indrawn breath of every Fair Weather-Maker around.

Plymouth gave a high-pitched wail.

'By Boreas, look!' shouted Dogger. 'To the West!'

They all drew in their breath sharply. What they saw was a terrifying spectacle, travelling towards them from over the sea.

'It's the Foul Weather-Makers' Extreme War Weather! They must have formed it from the Cabalistic signs in time,' cried the Wizard.

Their rejoicing choked in their throats.

For there, stretching over the entire horizon, for at least 80 miles … was an ominous Squall Line.

Composed of many Thunderstorms evenly spaced, it marched fearlessly onwards, ready to tumble rain over the British Isles forever.

'They've tricked us!' Forties bellowed, 'tricked us out of victory!'

'The War of the Weather isn't over at all!' cried Faeroes.

'Finisterre's advice was right,' cried Fastnet. 'But why isn't she here to help?'

Both Fronts had used exactly the same strategy: they'd cleverly destroyed one another's initial Defences … ready for their Extreme Weather to begin …

And the Fair Weather-Makers, stupidly thinking they'd won … found that this time …

THEY were the ones not ready.

171

Chapter 25
Nimbus the Thunderhead

The Squall Line approached like a myriad shadows marching abreast in pyramidal formation.

And set at its centrepiece, towering above all the rest against a leaden sky, stretching right into the stratosphere, was the biggest, blackest cloud any of them had ever seen. So fierce and jagged were its edges it knew no outline; so dense was it, that any light was swallowed into its depth.

Half creature, half machine, this cloud came rumbling straight towards them.

'NIMBUS! NIMBUS THE THUNDERHEAD!' breathed Wizard Wight.

Seeing the nightmare approach, Wendy yelled, 'What about me?' She knew that even if she were shot up to her former position, she'd not be higher than any tops of those advancing black clouds. And, because Fisher had asked for his *Absolutely Weatherproof* back, she'd be exposed in full view of the enemy, and wearing a very colourful Fair Isle jumper.

But nobody had time to begin setting up their Extreme Weather, and they already found themselves being pushed backwards by a strong Head Wind, which rocked the Altostratus cloud they were on.

'Pay attention everyone!' (King Faeroes voice was filled with anguish). 'We must form a new Front with everything we've got around us to protect our Castle. Collect together every cloud remnant. Work with what you can. Come on! Everything is urgent! Beaufort must be saved.'

Just then, a thin, mean, whining cross-wind was sent ahead by the enemy. It came blowing up as a kind of mocking calling-card, riding parallel to their rallying Front. It cleverly insinuated discontent among the ranks, nagging at their self-esteem. It worried annoyingly around Wendy's head.

So she decided to hide amongst the fluff.

Finding an Air-Pocket where no one could see her, she burrowed inside.

Faeroes chased the wind and quickly destroyed it. But it had performed its purpose in stalling their Warm Front's hurried re-building, and he realized this was yet another delaying tactic by the enemy … giving them no time. No time left to put any of their own Extreme Weather into action.

172

Again their King urged his troops, 'Don't be afraid! Be strong! We CAN fight harder and beat them! Use the power the tar has given us.'
... But, inside himself, Faeroes knew the situation was almost impossible: their 'vision of the future' was finished; their only hope of survival was to be Defensive. Finisterre had been right all along.

'Hurry!' he called again.

Soon, above Wendy's head, a massive weather-barrier was being built at an amazing pace.

Forties was intending to counteract Nimbus by hauling up a colossal mountain of Towering Cumulus. In vertical extent, this stretched to a massive 35,000 feet, descending in billows to only a few feet above sea-level.

Rockall and Fisher jumped into action, frantically positioning, along its highest reaches, a long line of protective Cirrus Castellanus with densely-rounded crenelated tops.

Streaking in every direction, Plymouth and Fastnet threaded, between these clouds, a fine trapping network of Cirrus Fibratus.

Dogger and Bailey were commanded to put an unyielding layer of Altostratus, reinforced with several strong Backing Winds as a buffer between that and the main cloud ... while Wizard Wight pushed in a Wedge of High Pressure, so strong that nothing, surely, would be able to shift it?

But all the while, ploughing furiously towards them, beset by tempestuous rumblings and swirling pockets of air, the Squall Line came hurtling along; each Storm-Cloud seeming neither to choose individual enemies, nor fight selectively.

Only Nimbus itself, like some massive war-tank, scattered everything in its path, sliding so low over the sea, that the ocean was lifted more than 20 feet above its normal level.

Its vast summit, like a giant's nose, was flattened into the shape of an anvil; and at its base, a menacing arch became an enormous mouth, waiting to engulf them.

With every cloud put in place, Faeroes ordered the Fair Weather-Makers to take cloud-cover off to one side, near to where Wendy was hiding on the large Altostratus. It was now all they could do.

Already winds, veering sharply, stung their faces, yet Faeroes hung on until he knew everyone was hidden.

Then, only after a huge wind-gust from the advancing Squall Line hit too hard, and the temperature dropped ten degrees suddenly, did he finally take cover himself.

All at once, Wizard Wight spoke up. 'Listen everyone. We have to attract Nimbus directly here – right towards our barrier. Only then can we be sure to destroy their centrepiece. And I have an idea.'

'What?' They needed every suggestion if they were to survive.

'By using Wendy as a lure. She has our Tome in her backpack, hidden by her from us all. It was inside her backpack when she arrived. I took it from her and hid it safely inside my Turret.

But now she's stolen it back from my Turret while we were watching my Light Show! That is why she suddenly disappeared. She's using our dire situation as an opportunity to escape with it over to Heligoland. Look where she cowers and hides away from us all inside an Air-Pocket!'

Then Wendy understood that the Wizard had kept a close watch on her all the time; marking her out while creating his Wedge of High Pressure.

'You dare treat her so!' Forties retorted; 'You'd be using the poor Earthling as a sacrifice!' He ran to put his great arms protectively around her.

But Fastnet, with her new tarry strength and greater speed, was already leaping over the fluff towards Wendy. None of them had known that the Earthling had brought the Tome with her – ready to use in her way. Beating Forties to it, Fastnet hauled her out of the Air-Pocket and snatched her up.

'She shall NOT escape over to the enemy with the Tome.'

Wendy's heart sank as the Wizard turned her around. She had no chance to explain to them that the Wizard had stolen the Tome from her for his own use: they would think it just a lame excuse.

The Wizard grabbed at her backpack, undid its clasps, whipped the dark green book from it and – held it up for all to see … just as it transformed its covers into a dark triumphant purple in his hands.

'Traitor! Betrayer!' they yelled.

Before she could recover from the shock, Wendy found herself wrenched again from the safety of Forties' arms as he battled against Fastnet to prevent her being sacrificed. Instead, her own arms were forced behind her back, then fastened strongly with Fisher's uncoiled sardine-catching line, which he always kept safely on his person.

Next, the Tome was strapped tightly in front of Wendy by winding several coils around her chest, then catching them together with the fishing-line's sardine-catching hooks at her back.

Wendy yelped helplessly as she was spun far out in front by Fisher, using a deft fly-fishing throw, and left dangling there.

She'd become a piece of tempting bait in full view of the oncoming giant – and, wearing the Mermaid's brightly-coloured Fair Isle pullover, making her still more exposed.

'See! The sight of the Tome, which Heligoland so badly wants returned, is held out to the enemy like a gift of appeasement,' grinned the Wizard. 'She's luring Nimbus right here – the only place where we can deal with it head on.' He chortled loudly at his clever plan, rubbing his hands together.

Inside this gigantic Thunderhead, the Foul Weather-Makers (who'd been blowing Nimbus along) had run into difficulties even before reaching the Warm Front.

Viking, its creator, crashed about, swearing in Norse. Warm air was needed desperately - to increase the saturation of their raindrops, and they had none.

Biscay and Hebrides were manufacturing fast-rushing cloud-columns and vapour-swirls from countless numbers of water-droplets; but, without any captured warm air, these would not be heavy enough to form into freezing hail to cause damage as they fell.

'Oh where is Captain Humber and his hail stones when we need them?' cried Hebrides.

Nimbus had all but reached the Warm Front, when Fair Isle, having a Mermaid's softer disposition, could no longer bear seeing the Earthling perish in this cruel way.

'I brought the tar to Beaufort myself … and now both sides are as Foul as each other,' she thought.

So, parting cloud-cover, Fair Isle disobeyed orders by galloping side-saddle (with her tail acting as a kind of anchor curled around her Wind-Force) right into the teeth of the gale. There, she expertly deposited a strong Spell of Hot Weather slap bang in front of the path of oncoming Nimbus, to lessen its impact on the dangling Earthling child.

Leaving a jet of hot shimmering air in her own path, she only just made it back before the giant black cloud burst through into her hot spell, juddered to a halt, and 'Hold on everyone!' she warned, as shock-waves from her action caused every cloud to rock dangerously - and Wendy to whimper in terror as she felt the huge yawning mouth sucking and sucking towards her.

She cringed, shutting her eyes tight, her body gone rigid with fear.

From the base of Nimbus, Hebrides announced suddenly, 'Look out! One of them's just thrown out a Spell of Hot Weather; dead ahead!'

Instead of being alarmed, German Bight gave a whoop.

'That's exactly what we need! Stop Nimbus immediately! Quick, Hebrides, suck up as much hot air as you can. At last we'll be able to make damaging hail.'

So, while German Bight ordered Malin to form a negative charge at the top of Nimbus, Hebrides and Biscay created a positive one at the bottom. Gradually, between them, they fashioned a magnificent generator, producing massive charges of electricity.

Soon electro-magnetic oscillations were shooting from one end of Nimbus to the other.

Into these, the Black Witch and Biscay cleverly threw their freshly-fashioned up-draughts of warm air and, as these currents hurtled skywards through the cloud, they met freezing temperatures controlled by Malin above.

Instantly the up-draughts condensed, turning into ice-drops which rose and fell, rose and fell, acquiring each time a further coating of ice.

Before long, the whole inside of Nimbus was jostling outsize balls of hail … with Viking left at the top, steering Nimbus with some difficulty in the anvil's summit.

Hebrides winced as hailstones rained down on her head.

'Hurry, Viking! Hurry!' she screamed. 'The hail's ready to fall. We're getting rattled to death down here!'

176

But Viking had spotted a tiny creature, hovering nervously behind the Mermaid's remaining heat-haze.

'By Thor himself, there's Lundy's little Helper, dead ahead - holding out our Tome to give back to us. We'll get them both – but she's tied to something,' he shouted down through Nimbus.

'Get them both, then. Now, Viking! Now!' Malin shouted

Viking gave a warlike bellow and hurled a burst of lightning down through Nimbus straight towards the bait.

The lightning zig-zagged past Wendy and the Tome, cleverly severing Fisher's fishing-line behind her in several places.

'Donner and Blitzen! That was magnificent!' cried German Bight. He was in his element, drunk with the glory of excess.

Wendy, her arms imprisoned by her sides and the book bound to her chest, found herself whirling downwards, tumbling straight towards the storm waves.

'Biscay, try to catch them before they sink!' Malin ordered.

'Use directional lightning, not zig-zag' – screamed Hebrides. 'Quick, before we lose our book altogether!'

Viking's second lightning-stroke of 10,000 degrees centigrade revealed, in one instance inside Nimbus, a boiling vision of walls, canyons, pinnacles and valleys. It whizzed past German Bight, narrowly missing Hebrides, and travelled straight on through the atmosphere towards the Earthling …

But, instead of separating Wendy from her book, his bolt hit the Tome smack bang in its centre, appearing to stay there in an electric plasma-storm whirling around itself.

An unearthly howling came from the Tome – hell-like - as a huge hole scorched right through the book's front cover, ripping each page asunder.

One after the other, these pages flew off in flames, as if the devil were reading the Tome at an alarming rate.

Every torn-off page squirmed into smelly, snake-like coils; then spasming and writhing, curled inwards to form bullet-balls of parchment.

These volcanic pellets whistled in small hard missiles, sizzling as they hit the water, screaming as they were shot below the waves.

There, their charred remains floated apart and disintegrated forever.

Wendy slumped forward over the Tome's empty back cover, then blacked out, leaving her body to follow the scorched pellets down, plummeting with them towards the waves.

At the same moment, Fair Isle flipped over their cloud for a second time. Performing a magnificent swallow dive with her tail curled around her Wind-force, she managed to catch the insensible Earthling in a swooping curve just before she hit the ocean.

This was quickly followed by Forties on his Wind-Force, rescuing both Earthling and Mermaid with a generous scoop of his hands, bringing them safely back to cloud-cover.

In Nimbus - Biscay had also left her position to catch the Tome. But she was too late ... and meanwhile, because her up-draughts stopped being thrown upwards by her, all the hailstones no longer held in suspension fell like a Storm-curtain, joining water with sky between both Fronts.

Like companion bullets they, too, crashed into the ocean, leaving Biscay returning to Nimbus empty-handed.

'Idiot! You've destroyed our precious Tome instead of the Earthling.' German Bight was beside himself with fury.

Hebrides cried, 'Move Nimbus forwards NOW. Kill the enemy, before we lose them as well!'

Nimbus reared upwards, curled back its upper lip, sucked up the hot air, and spat at their Front. It stretched forward, snatching fluff from the nearest clouds, embracing them in a wet stranglehold, then gulped them down.
After that, it went on the rampage.

Immense Wind-Pockets, blasting like cannon-fire, erupted from its bowels. Vortices, whirling off its anvil-shaped head, snorted from the innermost recesses of its snout.

At the same moment, it thundered into their Front.

Before it, further banks of white cloud cowered, parted, and edged sideways in defeat. Smaller clouds, hidden in their depth, scurried out trying to escape. Braver ones puffed themselves up and pulled in stray wisps.

Nimbus merely surrounded these with his cloud-fingers, pulling enemy fluff into his belly and, growing fatter, stormed onwards. He broke through the nets and threads of their cloud-wall, devouring a pathway through their defence.

The Fair Weather-Makers clung to one another, fearing they were doomed.

Viking, furious at his failure to save their Tome, spitefully created a vacuum inside Nimbus, into which vapour-packed air promptly poured. As this air smashed into itself from all sides, his Thunderbolts were released one after another like a firework display.

Each explosion rocketed down the lightning-path, tearing a track through cornfields, cracking convulsively into the ground. Then it thundered into their Towering Cumulus, forcing the whole lot backwards towards Beaufort; pushing their Castle cloud itself overland, with all its unused Extreme Weather still hidden behind.

Sole, who was waiting for this outburst, signalled to her auxiliary storms in the Squall Line on either side. A battery of lightning-strokes was followed by an extensive barrage of stinging rain. This fell in sheer sheets, sharp across the Southern coastline of the British Isles.

Biscay left Nimbus to blow Sole's rain in every direction, reaching, at her peak, Hurricane-Force winds.

Window-glass broke; greenhouses and fences shattered. Flower-gardens were crushed; crops destroyed … even Mr Allbright, the ex-Weather-man, took cover behind his Daily Mail at home ... for the computers had given warnings of gales from Force 9 to 12 in all sea areas - but hadn't forecast a hurricane. Opening his arms wide with helplessness, he spluttered 'I know in England hurricanes hardly happen … but they were wrong … entirely wrong! And this hurricane is huge!'

Sole's rain changed to hail, hail to sleet, then sleet to snow as the battlefield shifted further inland.

There were driving blizzards at the Lizard, drifts at Dungeness. Ships which had brazenly set out, went to anchor. Exceptional high tides shattered boats in harbours, lifting them well on to the land.

In that single day, four inches of rain fell on Maidenhead, and hailstones the shape and size of half-grapefruits fell on Surrey.

Only Eastbourne, being indebted to Beachy Head and the Chalk Downs for protection, and Bournemouth, similarly sheltered behind the Isle of Purbeck, got off scot-free.

Battered, shaken and displaced, the Warm Front was pushed uncomfortably almost onto Beaufort's own lawn behind them.

'If we don't do something soon,' Faeroes yelled, 'Our Castle will receive a complete Blow-out.'

Hebrides, cackling at their plight, left Nimbus when Biscay's Hurricane ended.

'Let our new Ice Age begin. This is FAR better than wrecking!'

Recklessly, she scooped up further supplies of defeated warm air and, giving the enemy up-draughts a quick twist ... as if she were wringing a sailor's neck ... used them to create a few Tornados.

The first sucked up bucketfulls of periwinkles and crabs, depositing them in Worcester High Street, forty miles from the sea.

The second surprised a man from Troubridge, who heard the sound of plopping behind him, and turned to see hundreds of tiny frogs falling from the sky.

The third Tornado, pointing towards the enemy's Castle, tore the roof off a very large Altostratus nearby. In one stroke it revealed, inside, all the Fair Weather-Makers rushing towards their Wind-Forces to escape ... just as, panic-stricken, the Fair Wind-Forces themselves broke loose and streaked emptily away.

Now they were left stranded - finally at the mercy of their enemy.

'Look! Now we've got'em!' Viking whooped triumphantly. 'And their Wind-forces have fled. And look, there's Windy ... we can pinch her back for Lundy as well!'

With that, they huffed the Altostratus forward to surround Beaufort Castle, so no-one could escape inside to take refuge.

Chapter 26
The Trough of Low Pressure

Wendy came to with a kind of electric buzzing throughout her body. 'I'm filled with electricity,' she announced, as the strong wind slapped her in the face. She sat up, feeling strangely above herself. The buzzing rays alerted her brain, making her full of Positive Thinking.

She looked around at the defeated Fair Weather-Makers, stranded and huddled together - with all their Wind-Forces blown away. She guessed that Beaufort Castle would get blown to smithereens next, and their stack of Extreme Fair Weather be discovered, then dismantled … poor Nanny and the children would get evaporated, too …

'No! They may be all defeated,' Wendy thought, 'but I'm not … not quite yet'… she knew exactly what to do.

She remembered clearly that one Wind Force hadn't blown away – one made ready for her earlier escape was tethered with Forties' windlass, under cloud-cover, at one edge of Beaufort's springy lawn.

Making her way through tattered cloud-tendrils to the edge of their diminishing Altostratus - and using the Foulest language she could muster - she called one of the small grey enemy clouds, which had been posted in position to surround this disintegrating enemy Altostratus, to come to her immediate aid.

The trembling enemy cloud obeyed her Foul language; so that Wendy was able to leap aboard and direct it to blow, in a scare-raising ride, the short distance onto the Westward part of Beaufort's rather crumpled lawn.

She leapt off the Foul cloudlet and ran towards the hiding-place. Yes! There was Finisterre's Backing Wind, still tethered with Forties' strong windlass, shivering and alone, hidden at the lawn edge exactly where she'd left it.

Undoing the windlass, Wendy jumped onto the Backing Wind. 'Blow away from here! Take me downwards towards Exeter,' she commanded.

At last she had escaped and was going back home.

As her Wind-Force blew along, bearing Wendy away from the disaster, she saw below her an enormous chunk of weather being pushed along by Sole the Doleful, using all her newfound tarry strength.

Sole had seen Nimbus spent and all its energy gone, so, once all her Thunderstorms were over, she'd collected the remaining Foul Weather from the Squall Line, and cleverly constructed with it -

A Trough of Low Pressure.

This she was pushing stealthily towards the disintegrating Altostratus that held the cowering Fair Weather-Makers ...

Carefully, she positioned her Trough directly beneath and waited for them to all fall in.

The Foul Weather-Makers were delighted and surprised at the doleful one's intelligent move. Now, they could just sit back and wait for the defeated Fair Weather-Makers to tumble into Sole's Trough, once they'd blown the Altostratus apart where all the Fair Weather-Makers were hiding.

After that, they'd dispose of the lot of them with one great smothering of Viking's strongest Sheet-Lightning.

Viking was the last to leave Nimbus. He looked at his structure sadly: it would finally collapse without him. He joined the others on their Wind-Forces in a line, along the edge of the Trough, waiting for their defeated Fair Weather-Makers to drop inside.

'Faeroes, save us!' whimpered Plymouth as the Fair Weather-Makers' cloud-edges started to evaporate.

'How can I without our Wind Forces? I'm afraid there's no hope left!'

Forties saw the enemy about to claim them, and shivered at the deep Trough below.

Fair Isle tried desperately to contact Finisterre using KR Magnetic 2 – but she could get no response.

Wizard Wight, however, seeing the enemy waiting ready for their final capture, thought up a way he could at least delay their end a little. Quickly, and with his remaining strength, he performed some gestures in the air to conjure up a little of their old-fashioned weather again: a mirage.

Magically, the mirage made their tattered cloud seem further than it really was, then nearer, then further again, wobbling the view of it in a scary dance.

The clever Wizard kept his illusion shifting, so that the confused Foul Weather-Makers had to keep moving their Trough around, ready to catch them …until Plymouth, who was incredibly far-sighted, yelled with all her might:

'Finisterre is coming to help. Look! At last!'

Racing through the Southern Skies in full battle-dress, her Coat of Arms emblazoned across her chest, the White Witch came galloping along on a Spanking Breeze. Behind her, with one hand, she pulled along the Azores High on a hundred strong Millibars, bringing with it a golden light, which spread right across Britain from the continental skies.

'I came as fast as I could!' Finisterre cried towards them. Then, seeing the urgency of the situation, she let go the Azores High and, pointing her fully-charged wand towards the remnants of their Altostratus cloud, created in one stroke, accompanied by a shower of falling sparkles, her best ever Rescue Remedy - an elegant Escape Bridge in glorious violet, indigo, blue, green, yellow, orange and red.

One by one, the Fair Weather-Makers, (with Faeroes carefully carrying his Mermaid on account of her slippery tail), climbed the Rainbow to safety.

The Foul Weather-Makers, seeing this terrible turn of events, leapt down quickly inside their own Trough to hide.

But it was freezing at its base – a spiteful trick Malin had planned, so that the captured Fair Weather-Makers would be unable to move.

'Oh!' Finisterre said, staring down into the Trough, and seeing only the frozen upturned eyes of the enemy Weather-Makers, glaring at her with fixed glassy hatred, as their thrashing around started to freeze them into stillness inside their own layer of frost.

However, when Finisterre rode over to talk to Faeroes, she saw, to her consternation, that all the Fair Weather-Makers had gone Foul as well. Tar had replaced the whites of their eyes – much as it had done to hers. (She'd arrived late because she'd needed to rid the tar from herself with some further Light Therapy at Portland Bill's.)

But then … What in the skies was happening?

The slippery Rainbow Bridge was already beginning to dissolve and fade in the heat of the Azores High.

And instead of strengthening her Rainbow, the White Witch decided on exactly the opposite procedure: she allowed her Rainbow to die away. And to the utter dismay of the Fair Weather-Makers, the White Witch - using Fitzroy's help - moved the Trough to position it right underneath where the Rainbow was fading …

… So then, as its Fine colours dissolved… all the Fair Weather-Makers were tumbled in on top of the Foul.

Now Finisterre sighed, knowing that she alone held complete
Authority of the Skies.
So quickly, she pronounced their fate.

'It's to be like this: you're all to be sent to the Doldrums to be properly becalmed. Only once you're cleansed of any tar will you be returned to your Castles in the Sky … There, you will endeavour to produce a proper balance of some Fair and some Foul weather as you used to do.'

Their sentence pronounced, Finisterre instructed the Azores High to push the heavy Trough of Low Pressure, filled full with its mixture of Weather-Makers, slowly and steadily along to the Doldrums.

After that, Finisterre looked into the distance, and she noticed, far away, the fleeing speck of the Earthling on her own Backing Wind, blowing from them as hard as the poor thing was able.

But the White Witch had not finished with the Earthling, just yet.
Putting her two lips together, she blew, whistling shrilly across the skies.

Her Backing Wind, hearing its Mistress's summons, reared in delight, stopped short - nearly throwing its rider - changed direction sharply, then blew rapidly back towards its rightful owner.

And Wendy found herself returning exactly the way she'd come - her escape foiled yet again; her excellent plan demolished.

'I deserve to be allowed to go back home to Earth,' she explained tearfully to Finisterre, her voice filled with disappointment. 'I was almost destroyed using the Tome … but the Tome got destroyed instead.'

Finisterre caught her Backing Wind by its reins, and held it still … 'Well I'm extremely relieved that you did, Wendy. You must have realized by now that the Tome tempted ignorant people to achieve power, using it to the detriment of others – and waiting to destroy even the planet itself.'

Then taking Wendy gently by the shoulders, Finisterre looked into her eyes.

She saw in them an Earthling who was a changed person: much troubled; older-looking – yes - far more grown up.

She'd suffered War-Damage - but at least there was no tar inside her eyes. The White Witch was pleased about that. The Earthling looked Fair enough now, both after her bad time at Heligoland then her anti-Fouling at Beaufort ... or did she?

The White Witch wasn't fooled. She stared deeper into the Earthling girl's eyes.

Wendy stared back into Finisterre's clear blue ones.

'Help me, Finisterre,' she pleaded. 'I think I'm still half Foul - and half Fair. I feel so changeable - like two people at once.'

'Like me,' Finisterre reassured. 'We're two of a kind ... it can be difficult ... but not impossible. Fitzroy is working with me currently, thanks to Portland Bill's help – not against me. Tell me, Wendy, could you go back home and live with what you've become?'

'Y... yes ... I suppose I could ... but ...'

'You do see now that there has to be some Fair and some Foul weather to balance the world. Not Extreme Weather caused by oil – nor coal for that matter. Both give the planet pollution ... and Pollution is not the solution.

It's really left to you mortals ... but you all have a chance now that the Tome's been destroyed. So thank you for seeing to that.'

'But I need you to see what the future might hold for you Earthlings, if you go on allowing the Extreme Weather to persist.

'You see I experienced an Epiphany ... a kind of revelation if you like ... while undergoing Light Therapy at Portland to cure the tar in myself.

This Epiphany allowed me to understand, with exquisite clarity, what could lie ahead if the air was choked with greenhouse gases.

Now look deeply, Wendy – for I want you to really understand, with this same clarity, what would happen if each of you Human Beings persists in your pollution.

'So, I'm granting you an Epiphany yourself. Concentrate hard.'

Wendy did, and she saw in great detail what would happen if the **Fair**

Weather-Makers had won the War of the Weather:

Working at Extreme High Pressure, the earth would be tormented with heat-waves. Forest fires would crackle and get out of hand; dust devils dance across the land.

The scorched earth would turn fields into crazy dried puzzle-chunks; rivers, canals and wells would dry up, ponds, streams and waterfalls trickle sadly to a stop; crops go to waste, cattle lowing, sheep bleating sadly...

Spring's song-birds would waste away; trees wither, infested with pests and disease.

Next, Wendy visualized *the seas heating up, pumping warmed moisture into the air. This warm water would expand, forcing sea-levels to rise. Waves would crash against the shores, somersaulting houses over the edges of cliffs; tumbling the cliffs down themselves.*

Worse would come; **Extreme Fair Weather** *could twist warmer skies into typhoons, hurricanes and tornados, bringing tidal waves so high that they'd swamp both people and homes, put low-lying coastal cities at risk, and, by invading low-lying lands, would salt up and spoil the fields for both crops and grass-lands.*

Much lower, deep inside the oceans, colder currents would warm up, too, and begin to flow in new directions, jiggling the jet-stream above, melting icebergs like lollipops in the sun, destroying many sea-creatures and their habitats forever.

The White Witch screwed her eyelids shut, then opened them wide again for Wendy to look a second time. Now she saw what the **Foul Weather-Makers would cause if they won:**

There'd be Cold Arctic air plunging temperatures for days on end; severe storms with deadly lightning strokes; winds of over 100 mph. Electricity power lines would be cut off; phone-lines go down; houses suffer with frozen burst pipes; lorries overturned in high winds.

There'd be increasing snowstorms causing airports to close; cars to break down; trains to get stuck; people stranded or slipping on the ice - hospital admittances rising.

Most of all, rain would come pouring; more and more of it, lashing down for days on end from endless thunderstorm-skies. It would wash good soil into the seas and drown any houses on low-lying land.

Flash floods would burst river-banks, bloating them with litter. Broken branches, plastic bags, and human detritus plucked by the waters, would charge on by.

Cattle and sheep, pigs and hens would get diseased and die ....

'So you see, Wendy, Extreme weather is very different from our usual weather patterns. Your pollution is even now making oceans more acid, so that seashells can no longer build their shells, and corals bleach and decay.

'There has to be equal proportions - some Fair, some Foul … that is, if you want your world to go round.'

'How will I do that?'

'You mean what is the solution to the problem. Quite easy: all you need is the mind to do it. So, go back down to Earth …

Teach everyone that the air is choking on an abundance of poisonous gases in the atmosphere.

Stop disturbing your ground: fracturing it with fracking, building dams, altering water-courses and rivers.

Leave oils and coals inside the ground.

Use wind, sun, photosynthesis, waste-materials and the natural motion of the seas for your energy.

Cut down on your cows, sheep, pigs and hens – they pollute as well as you.

Variety is good: plant more trees and hedges, sow wild flowers; have ponds, keep marshes un-drained … get rid of your plastic bags which fishes choke on.

Warn the world, Wendy. It's nearly too late!

Perhaps there should not be so many of you … ???

The White Witch put her arms around Wendy and hugged her. 'You're ready to go now. We've both made sacrifices … and there are still far more to be made. I'll help you up here if I can, responding to what you do down on earth.'

Then, pointing her wand at Wendy, she sent her floating slowly downwards in calm conditions, to teach a new way of living to the world.

As Wendy fell, she felt herself growing heavier, making her fall faster, so that by the time the wind-sock on the Meteorological Office in Exeter caught her, sliding her gently down onto its roof – she was back on Earth and into her own weight again.

The following day, by the time the morning star had arisen, trembling with apprehension, and a blushing rose-coloured dawn faded quickly from view, the Azores High worked to start a great thaw throughout the country.
Soon, the battle-torn skies were cleared.
Then everyone's spirits were lifted as they tidied up and swept the mud away from their doors.
'**The War of the Weather** is over,' the people of Britain said as they climbed into bed.

Post script.

THE SHIPPING FORE-CAST ... once it's Weather-Makers were becalmed.

Finisterre, after receiving a final Light Therapy Boost by Portland Bill, was able to separate herself from Fitzroy completely, so she generously left him her Sea Area to manage on his own.
Finisterre, herself, was invited back to Beaufort as Cordon Bleu Cook, while Sunny Intervals was kept as a holiday home, looked after by the Kittiwake Family and the Curlews.
After lifting the spell on Fisher's rod, the White Witch could choose to have a greater variety of unendangered fish species for her gorgeous recipes.
Then Finisterre and Fisher got married, with a reception on Beaufort's re-landscaped lawn – with Nanny Dover throwing Ambrosia rice on the married couples' heads.
Fisher took his bride on a honeymoon using the Jet Stream, and flew with her twice around the world.
'What a Fine way to travel,' Finisterre remarked. 'I'll always fly this way now; it's so convenient and quite takes the breath away.'
Finisterre's portrait was turned the right way up again in the Long Gallery... and, before long, a further miniature portrait added ... for Finisterre had given birth to Trafalgar – who was already turning out to be a

little Castle Genius, sitting there on his own High chair, tending properly to fluctuate from High to Low.

But although Finisterre remembered to becalm Nanny Dover and the Children, she completely forgot about sending Lundy away for therapy.
However, after receiving the Heligoland Inhabitants back with an extended ladle, Lundy showed them that she'd had been busy in her own way during their absence, with a surprise for the Thunderer.
'Here you are, Viking. This is little North Utsire and this is little South Utsire,' she announced, pressing the Foul twins into his unsuspecting arms.
Viking blushed with delight as he cradled one in each arm … 'And now you'll 'ave to make an honest woman of me, won't you – after all that cavorting with me inside the Heligoland Sugar-bin …'
Lundy had already turned Malin's old room into a nursery, with little cold showers, two little cloud-cots and a small roller for wringing out cloud-nappies.
However, she soon found the Foul Weather-Makers a little too calm, so, by regulating her cooking, was able to whip them up into better shape again.

Count and Countess Bight (with Toad) moved into the North Turret together. Soon they produced a little Foul one of their own, called Cromarty … who would grow up to be a new Foul Wizard at Heligoland Hall.

From then onwards, the Fair Weather-Makers lived happily ever after … and the Foul Weather-Makers lived unhappily ever after … which is mostly what they preferred.

As for Wendy - she was greeted with relief and delight by her mother and friends. She pursued a Degree in Climatology, then a Doctorate in Global Affairs, and worked unceasingly to change the Earthlings' attitude to the planet.
And many people really tried to change their way of life, knowing that if they did so individually, it would all add up.

The End